# OUT WEST AND BACK

## Charles C. Fletcher

Published By
FLETCHER BOOKS

© 2007 by Charles C. Fletcher.
All rights reserved. No part of this book may be reproduced, stored in a retrieval system or transmitted in any form or by any means without the prior written permission of the publishers, except by a reviewer who may quote brief passages in a review to be printed in a newspaper, magazine or journal.

Second printing

All characters in this book are fictitious, and any resemblance to real persons, living or dead, is coincidental.

ISBN: 978-1-933251-76-9

Published By
## Fletcher Books
2310 Harris Circle NW
Cleveland, TN 37311

Printed in the United States of America

# CONTENTS

| | |
|---|---|
| INTRODUCTION | 7 |
| OUT WEST AND BACK | 9 |
| THE NEW SCHOOL | 13 |
| GROWING UP | 17 |
| NEIGHBORS | 22 |
| DIGGING THE WELL | 26 |
| AN AIRPLANE RIDE | 30 |
| MODEL A FORD | 32 |
| CCC CAMP | 37 |
| VIRGINIA | 44 |
| DRAFTED | 51 |
| THE WAR | 59 |
| GETTING MARRIED | 64 |
| RAISING A FAMILY | 70 |
| MOVING TO TENNESSEE | 75 |
| THE PAPER MILL | 79 |
| CLEVELAND | 85 |
| RETIRED | 99 |
| GRANDCHILDREN | 111 |
| LIVING ALONE | 116 |
| SHORT STORIES | 121 |
|    OLD RED, THE ROOSTER | 121 |
|    OLD RED AND THE WORM | 123 |
|    OLD RED AND THE NEW ROOSTER | 124 |
|    CHICKEN AND DUMPLINS | 126 |
|    A ROOSTER FOR DINNER | 128 |

| | |
|---|---|
| MY DOG AND THE BOBCAT | 131 |
| BLACKBERRY COBBLER | 135 |
| CHRISTMAS, 1933 | 137 |
| BASEBALL IN THE 1930s | 142 |
| THE MULE | 145 |
| FIREPLACE COOKING | 149 |
| FUN TIME IN THE 1930s | 152 |
| MY ENGLISH VACATION, 1944 | 157 |
| MY BIRTHDAY, 1944 | 165 |
| THE PICNIC | 169 |
| UNCLE BOB | 173 |
| AUTHOR'S NOTES | 180 |

# INTRODUCTION

*Out West and Back* is an account of the brighter side of a poor mountain boy's growing up. The full story of my life is not included, only the lighter side of my experiences. All events and names are true to the best of my knowledge except where I have noted.

*Out West* starts when our home and all of our belongings were lost in a fire. It was one night in the year of 1927 when my mother was awakened about two A.M. by smoke in our bedroom. She got my sister, brother, and me and pushed us out of the burning house just before the roof fell in.

My father's mother (Grandma) operated a boarding house, and we went there. The next morning my parents sent a telegram to my mother's dad (Grandpa) who had a ranch and farm in Greeley, Colorado. He sent us train tickets so that we could come live with him. This was the start of "out west and back" for me.

This happened during the Great Depression when there was no work for anyone and no market for the crops or cattle that Grandpa raised. To Grandpa, this left only one thing to do: sell at any price, move back to the mountains of Western North Carolina, and start over again. He had sold his mountain land (Pressley Mountain) in Haywood County, North Carolina, to get money to buy the Colorado land. My family stayed in Colorado after Grandpa left.

In 1929 Mother was begging Dad to move back East. Dad gave in to Mom's nagging and some way came up with enough money to buy a used Model T Ford car complete with curtains. This was the start of the "and back" portion of my story.

CHARLES C. FLETCHER

I recorded the events in this story after many questions from my children and grandchildren about what took place during my lifetime. I took up their challenge although I am now nearing my 85th birthday.

You can now read part of my story, *Out West and Back*, but the "and back" part will not be complete because I am still on the trip back.

## OUT WEST AND BACK

I was about five years old when this part of my life began. The following events are accurate to the best of my knowledge.

In the year of 1927 we were living (my family and I) in Gastonia, North Carolina. Gastonia was one of the larger cotton mill towns in the South. My dad worked on the night shift in a cotton mill that was called Loray Mills. (The name is Firestone today.) We lived in one of the company houses that the factory furnished to their employees.

One night my brother, my sister, my mother, and I were at home sleeping when at about 2:00 A.M. my mother was awakened by the smell of smoke. She managed to push, pull, and shove until we children were out of the house—just in time. The whole house was engulfed in flames.

My Grandmother (my father's mother) had a boarding house across town. Someone took us to her place. We had no clothing or any other belongings. Everything had gone up in smoke.

My mother's family (five brothers, one sister, Mother, and Father) were living in Greeley, Colorado, at this time. My dad's mother sent a telegram to Grandpa Pressley telling him about what had happened. He wanted us (my family) to come stay with them. He had a very large ranch where he had cattle and also farmed. He grew sugar beets, potatoes, and pinto beans.

Grandpa Pressley sent us train tickets to use to come to Colorado. Off we went, westward bound. We lived there until the fall of 1929.

We got all the crops in, but we had no one to sell to. If someone did buy something, they only paid about half what it was worth. There was no market for anything. No one had any money to buy the things they needed. All people about my age can recall the Great Depression. We weren't poor—we were the same as everyone else. Everyone was poor.

Grandpa decided to sell out and head back east. He had lost his mountain in North Carolina (Pressley Mountain near Canton, North Carolina, in the Stamey Cove area), but he planned to buy a smaller place and find work for himself and his boys.

Dad stayed behind and was working for a Mr. Green. He furnished us a house to live in and milk, meat, and other food supplies to keep us from being hungry.

Most women want to be close to their mom, dad, sisters, and brothers. My mom was no exception. She said, "Let's go back to North Carolina." So, after a few weeks, Dad took what money he had and bought a Model T Ford to use for traveling. It was a sedan, and it had snap-on curtains. It didn't cost much. The owner couldn't buy gasoline for it (at 12 cents a gallon), so he sold it to Dad.

Out went the back seat. Mom packed her keepsakes (quilts, towels, pictures, etc.) in the space where the seat had been. This was to be seat, bed, and home for my brother, my sister, and me for the trip back East.

Preparations were made. Dad killed 10 or 12 ring-neck pheasants, and Mom packed them in salt in a pot. This would feed us for a few days. Dad also made sure he had plenty of rivets and clutch lining material for the car. We didn't pack any household belongings. We just left them. We couldn't sell anything.

So, off we went. The first few days went very well. We had to stop at least once a day to eat. Dad would gather sage brush, sticks, or anything that would burn and make a fire. Mom cooked; we ate; and then we were back on the road again.

In the year 1929, there were no motels, filling stations, or eating places along the way except in the larger towns. Also, there were no bridges over the rivers—only ferry boats. The roads in 1929 were very few and narrow, some being dirt roads, and they were not maintained very well. We had to stop about every 50 to 75 miles for Dad to re-line the clutch on the car. How long the clutch would last would vary, depending on whether we were traveling over flat roads or hills.

And there were the rivers to cross. This part was not as easy as one might think because there were no bridges over the rivers, and some were very wide or deep or both. The only way across was by ferry boats. We had a close call one night crossing a river. As Dad would drive day and night, and the lights on the T Model were not too bright; he had to be alert all the time. My brother, sister, and I were asleep in the back seat of the car when all at once I heard my mom scream, "Stop! Stop!"

Dad managed to get the car stopped, and not a moment too soon. The front wheels of the car were nearly in the water of the Missouri River at the ferry landing. Dad kept his foot on the brake, and Mom jumped out and somehow in the dark found a large rock to scotch the rear wheel to keep us from rolling into the water.

Dad started looking for the ferry. Finally he saw a light on the other side of the river. It looked like it was miles away. Dad began to whistle and holler trying to get the operator's attention. At last we saw the light moving toward us in the far distance. After what seemed a lifetime, the ferry was docked in front of our car. Mom removed the rock from the wheel, and Dad drove onto the ferry. All of this happened sometime after midnight. Mom was a very religious person, and I believe until this day that we were saved from a sure death for some reason that I can't explain.

Another scary thing that I remember happened at night also. Dad had parked the car on the side of the road to get a few minutes of sleep. He was sleeping when all at once a hand parted the curtains and was on Dad's face. He hollered real loud, opened the door, and got out. Someone was running away as fast as he could go. Dad was convinced that it was someone looking for food. He didn't know that we were in the car. No one was hurt, just a little excited. Dad didn't continue his nap; he started up the Ford, and we were on our way again.

Soon the food we had brought along with us was all gone. We had to wait to eat until we came to a town or store where we could restock with canned goods. Also, we had to refill the gas cans that we carried in order to have enough gasoline to get between filling stations. I guess that Dad knew the route to take sort of like the birds do. He didn't have any maps to go by.

I can't believe we made such a trip under such conditions. Dad drove night and day, only stopping a few hours each day to catch a cat-nap. I still think about the many times we had to holler and blow the car horn to get a ferry to come take us over a river. Five days—Where are we? Eight, nine, ten, eleven days—We are in North Carolina.

I didn't try to fill in all the details, only the highlights of that eleven-day-and-night trip. All that I've told here is a true account. I know—I was six years old.

# THE NEW SCHOOL

    We were getting settled down, and everything was getting back to normal when Mom informed me that school was to start soon, and I was to start all over. I started going to school while in Colorado but never finished the lower part of 1st grade. In 1929 there were two 1st grades in school: lower 1st (Primer) and upper 1st (the "real" 1st). The Primer was the equivalent of the kindergarten we have today (2007).

    The school was pretty close to where we were living and really close to my great aunt, Grace Smathers. Her second husband, "Uncle Rufe" Smathers, had donated the land for the school many years earlier. It was a two-room school—one room for the lower grades and another room for the higher grades. It had only two teachers. Each room had a large coal-burning heater that the students had to keep going (burning). We had to take turns bringing coal from under the school for the heater.

I didn't want to go to that school, but it seemed that all mothers wanted their children to get an education. The fathers seemed to think working was more important than going to school.

If we were punished for not obeying the rules at school, we had to go to the woods and cut the hickory switch that would be used to punish us. We would put a ring around the switch with a knife. This would make it break easy, and the whipping would not last too long.

I didn't have to go to this school very long. A new modern school was built at Beaverdam, and I went there. I don't recall how many rooms it had, but there were six grades, each having its own room. The new school also had an auditorium for morning announcements and a daily prayer.

There was also a full-time employee hired to keep the coal-fired furnace going and to keep the building clean. His name was Burt Robinson. He kept a good supply of candy on hand in the furnace room to sell to the lucky students who happened to have a penny or nickel to spare. Not too many had any money. He also kept the wooden floors in the school mopped with used motor oil. The oil was used for several reasons. It kept the floors clean; it preserved the wood; and it kept the bugs, ants, and other insects away as well as the field mice from the woods.

Many students were very poor. There were several who came without anything to eat at noon. We were taught to share with them. My lunch was usually left-overs from what we had to eat the night before or for breakfast. I carried this in a half gallon "Soco" lard bucket. We were lucky—my brother and I did eat.

There was lot of difference between the old two-room school (Austin Chapel School) and the new school (Beaverdam Elementary School). At the old school, you had to get to school any way you could. At the new school, you could ride the state-operated bus if you lived at least one mile away from the school. If you lived less than a mile away, you walked to school. The walking students were probably healthier than those who rode the bus because of the exercise that they got.

It was decided that I should start in the same grade as my brother, TJ. This would save money because we could share the same books, paper, pencils, or anything else that was needed. It worked pretty well, but this caused me to be a grade behind for my age—TJ was a year and six months younger than me.

Many things happened at this new school over the next few years.—I won't tell all that took place, only a couple of things.

Baseball was one of the top sports with all the boys then. This was true at Beaverdam in the year 1930. We needed a baseball field, but the land available was covered with tree stumps. Back in those days there were no bulldozers to use to clear a site. Trees were cut and moved with horses, and the tree stumps remained in the ground. How would these stumps be removed?

Our school principal was a Mr. Barbee. He had an idea: instead of the usual punishment for the boys, their punishment would be to dig up a stump. Sometimes they had to dig up more than one, depending on what the offense was. The bad part of digging the stumps was that you had to do the digging on your own time—after school in the evenings or on a Saturday (no Sunday work). I guess I did my share of clearing stumps for the ball field.

One boy (I'll just call him "Sorrels") was given three stumps to dig. I don't know what he did to get so many, but, anyway, he had the perfect plan. He lived on upper Beaverdam Creek at the foot of the mountain. His dad owned a corn mill and did some farming. He, too, had to remove stumps in order to have a place to plant his crops. He cleared his fields the easy way: he blew the stumps out with dynamite. Well, this Sorrels boy knew all about "the easy way" to remove stumps.

It happened on a Friday. The Sorrels boy didn't ride the bus home. He stayed around until everyone was gone. It wasn't long until his three stumps were out of the ground. I don't know how much dynamite he brought to school or how he hid it from the other students all day long, but he got the job done "the easy way." Well, come

Monday, Mr. Barbee checked the ball field. It so happened that he knew a little about digging and blasting. He called Sorrels to the office and asked about the stumps. Like most mountain people, Sorrels wouldn't tell a lie, so the truth came out, and he was given three more stumps to remove.

One fall, the weather was very bad for several days—rain, wind, and cold. A flock of wild ducks was forced to settle down in a field along the creek near the school. My teacher was named Mrs. King. (She was everyone's favorite teacher.) She saw the ducks and said, "I would like to have one of those ducks for Sunday dinner." Well, all the boys always carried a sling-shot (called a "flip" in Tennessee). One of the other boys and I volunteered to kill her a duck, and she gave us permission to go duck hunting. We headed to the creek, and all the wild ducks flew away. It so happened that there was a nearby farmer who had some tame ducks, and it so happened they were in the creek—Well, everyone knows that a good hunter always brings something home with him when he goes hunting, so we killed one of the farmer's tame ducks and gave it to Mrs. King. She never knew that the duck we gave her was a tame one and not the wild one she sent us after.

I was at Beaverdam Elementary School through the sixth grade. My brother and I then had to change schools. Our school had its ball field before we left for the seventh grade.

# GROWING UP

I am sure that every boy pushes himself toward manhood so he can own the things that are allowed after a certain age. When he has these things he can hang out with the big boys. I was no exception. For example, I had to get me a gun that belonged to me and no one else. Also, there were other things: a Barlow pocket-knife, your own hunting dog, your own chickens, and other things for use around the farm that would make you feel that you were contributing something to the family.

I happened to have a pretty good knife (not a Barlow), a few chickens, and a small, feist dog that would run a rabbit and sometimes tree a possum. The two things I wanted most were my own shotgun and a blue-tick or red-bone hound dog. (These were supposed to be the best dogs.)

For several months I had been looking at a gun in the hardware store window in downtown Canton. The price was twelve dollars (no tax). I had never had that much money in my lifetime. The most I had ever had was maybe one or two dollars. After all, there wasn't too much work for a twelve-year-old boy (or anyone else), as times were still bad after the Depression. If you found work, the pay was only ten cents (10¢) an hour, so twelve dollars was big money seventy-plus years ago.

I wasn't about to give up on getting that gun—No siree. So, one day I happened to have two whole dollars in my overalls pocket, and I got up enough nerve to go into the hardware store and ask for some sort of a deal for me to buy that beautiful gun. The owner of the store asked me how much money I had. Hanging my head down and looking at the floor, I said, "Two dollars."

"Know when you'll have more money?" he asked.

"No, sir," I said. "Don't get to work much seeing that I go to school and can only work in the evenings and on Saturday. But I can work more when school is out this summer."

"I'll make a deal with you," said the store owner. "You give me the two dollars you have, and pay me as much as you can when you do get to work."

The whole world lit up. I felt like I was floating on air. "Yes, sir," I said. "I'll do everything I can to pay you soon. And, uh, uh...I'll need some shells for my gun."

"You can have one box, and that will add another fifty cents to your bill," he told me. "You will owe me ten dollars and fifty cents."

"Yes, sir. I shore thank you for trusting me. If anything should happen that I can't pay you, I'll bring the gun back, and you can keep the two dollars I gave you today," I said.

Boy, oh boy. I had my own gun. I went walking out of the store with the box of shells in one hand and the gun on my shoulder so everybody could see it. And off I went, straight for home to show the gun off there. Was I excited? You bet. I was looking forward to heading to the mountains to shoot squirrels or any other wild animal that I came across.

The days went by awfully slow that week. The next Saturday was to be my first hunt with my new gun. I had been hunting many times with my dad. He was a dedicated hunter who went every time that he could, and I often went along with him. But, this would be my first time alone with my own gun.

Saturday morning I got out of bed at four-thirty. I didn't sleep very much the night before, thinking of the trip I planned. I knew the exact spot that I was going to go to—a grove of hickory nut trees about halfway up Little Sam Mountain. I had been there before with my dad. There were always squirrels there early every morning. Hickory nuts are very hard, and squirrels love them for two reasons. One is that they are very good food, and the other is that squirrels keep their teeth worn down by gnawing them. Squirrels' teeth grow very fast throughout their entire life-time. If they didn't keep their teeth worn down, their teeth would grow too long. Another is that hickory nut trees are the perfect place to hunt for squirrels.

It was very dark when I left the house and headed up the mountain. I had been to the spot several times and knew the right trail to take. The five-thirty whistle at the paper mill blew, and daylight was beginning to break through. I only had a little ways to go. Soon I was there, sitting on the side of the mountain above the hickory nut trees. I had a perfect view of every thing down the mountain. Everything was very quiet.

Then I heard a noise in the leaves. Something was coming up the spring branch. I knew it wasn't a squirrel—they travel through the trees. Finally, I saw something coming straight up the trail toward me. I cocked the gun and set the sights on whatever it was. It kept coming toward me. It was light enough to see that it was not a dog. I couldn't see what color it was. I followed it with my gun while it came closer and closer. Bang. I hit him, and down the mountain side he rolled, kicking and making a blood curdling cry.

I reloaded the gun and began to go down slowly to see what it was. The animal was still when I reached the spot where it lay. I could see that it was dead. I turned it over with my foot, and then I knew what I had killed. It was a big male mixed-breed fox, half red fox and half grey fox. There were many fox hunters in the mountains of North Carolina, and they never killed foxes. They only let their dogs chase them for sport. If you killed a fox and they found out, you would lose many of your friends forever.

I removed my coat, folded it around the fox, put him over my shoulder, and headed down the mountain. I was going home. There was no need to stay because the noise I had made scared the squirrels so bad that they moved to the next hollow.

After showing the fox to my family, I took him out back of the wood shed and began the tedious task of skinning him. I had to be very careful not to damage the hide. If it were damaged, it wouldn't bring a good price when I sold it. Soon I was finished and had a perfect pelt.

I even removed the bone from the tail. After rubbing salt on the inside of the skin (this was to keep the flies away), I picked a good spot on the wood shed wall to hang the hide for curing. I planned to ship it off along with a few possum hides I already had.

About four weeks later, I carefully packed the fox hide along with the ones I had from the possums and mailed them to a buyer in New York City. I had found his address in the *Saturday Evening Post*, a small weekly newspaper that nearly everyone depended on for the news. It wasn't long before I received a check in the mail for my hides—one dollar and twenty-five cents for the fox, one dollar and twenty cents for a big white possum hide, and fifteen to twenty cents each for the other ones. This would make a good payment on my gun.

I had many other hunting trips after that first one. Also, many strange things happened while I was hunting, but nothing serious. Some of the incidents were very funny; some were sad. About one year later the gun belonged to me. I had made the last payment on my twelve-dollar gun.

The growing-up part of this book wouldn't be complete without telling about one of the houses that we lived in. This house was located in the section that was known by the name "Thickety." I don't know why this name was chosen or who chose the name. It was an area along the foot of Little Sam Mountain. Most all the houses around there were about one mile or more apart, but we called each other "neighbors."

The house we lived in was known as the "Willis House." Mr. Carr Willis, one of the early settlers of this area, had the house built. We were the second or third generation to live in it. The house was large for its time. It had three bedrooms (sleeping rooms), a living room (parlor), and a very large room that was the kitchen and dining room together. All of the rooms had inside doors so you could enter any one of them from the inside. There was also an exterior door to each room for an exit to the porch that ran the full length of the house. When we asked why the house had outside doors, we were told that these were added so that if there was a fire everyone could get out of the house safely.

The Willis House was heated with a wood-burning stove in the kitchen and a Franklin wood-burning heater in the living room. All the other rooms had no heat. The house was constructed on the outside with weather boarding, and the inside was walled with wood paneling.

There was no running water or any electric lighting in the house. Our water came from a hand-dug well attached to the kitchen section of the house. For lighting at night, we used kerosene lamps. The toilet was a wooden building located in the field away from the house. For toilet tissue we usually used pages torn from a sales catalog or newspaper.

Our bathing facilities were also quite crude. There were two choices: you went to the nearby creek and braved the cold mountain water, or you drew water from the well and used a large wash tub in one of the back rooms. I preferred the creek. "City people" were always telling that we country folks only bathed once a week. This was incorrect. We bathed nearly every day; we only changed the water once a week.

As for eating, we did pretty well. We would kill squirrels, rabbits, and other game for part of our meat. We had chickens for eggs and would eat one of the chickens sometimes. Eating chicken was a treat and reserved for Sunday mornings. We would have fried chicken, saw-mill gravy, cooked apples, big pieces of "hand patted" butter, and biscuits. Sometimes one of the neighbors would kill a beef and go from house to house selling what he didn't need. He usually charged ten cents a pound regardless of what part you wanted. We also raised one or more hogs for our winter meat. We would pack the meat in salt to preserve it. We had a cow for our milk and butter. My mother would take some of the rich cream from the top of the milk and save it. About once each week she would churn the cream to make butter. She had a wooden butter mold that she used. The butter would come out round with a pretty flower molded on the top.

All of this was a small part of growing up for me.

# NEIGHBORS

Back when I was growing up, the word, "neighbor," meant more than it does today. Today we refer to the people who live in our neighborhood as our "neighbors," but are they? A very few are real neighbors; the other ones are just people who live close to where you have your house. They never visit or offer to give you a hand when you need someone to help you do a task that you can't do by yourself. They only take care of "number 1"—themselves.

In the community where I grew up, everyone was a real neighbor. You didn't have to ask someone to give you a hand when you needed help. Neighbors were always looking for ways to help someone who needed help. These were true neighbors. Their help was given without any expectations of payment for their services.

Communication was pretty good in the mountains of western North Carolina although we didn't have phones, and very few families had a car. We traveled on foot or by horse and delivered news by word-of-mouth.

We knew when someone died in the community: the bell at the church would toll. We usually knew who had died because we would hear if someone was seriously sick when we went to church services on Sunday. So, when that bell rang at the church, several people would get their mattocks and shovels and head to the church graveyard. We knew there was a grave to be dug. We never thought of asking for pay to dig graves. This was being a neighbor.

I dug or helped dig many graves. They had to be the exact length, width, and depth. The sides were as smooth as glass. Vaults were not used. Digging a grave back then was an art. Not everyone could dig a decent one.

Another example of neighborliness occurred when the Baptists of our community decided that we needed a decent building to hold worship services in. Services had been held in the old Cabe, one-room school house. A building committee was appointed, and plans were made to begin building a new church building.

The location chosen was near the existing graveyard. On the site was a grove of oak trees that had to be removed before building could begin. My family volunteered to get the trees out of the way. My brother, TJ, and I provided the labor for digging up the tree stumps. We didn't have any dozers or other earth moving equipment in the 1930s. It was all hand work.

We didn't have too much trouble with the smaller trees, but there was a huge red oak that refused to come up. The tap-root was large and grew straight down. We needed help. "Dink" Wines (my well-digging buddy's brother) and my dad came to our rescue. One evening after they came home from work, they placed dynamite under the tree root. We stood at a safe distance, and after a loud boom, our tree was out of the ground.

I did lots of other work building the church, like helping dig the basement. We used horses to pull the plows and scoop pans. It was slow, but everyone was patient.

The building started taking shape. Rock and brick masons were hired. A carpenter supervisor was hired to oversee building the church structure. When I later helped the builders, I was paid 10¢ (ten cents) an hour.

Soon the building was completed, with a bell tower, a basement, and a beautiful sanctuary for church services. Everyone was proud of this new church. Its name was "Oak Grove Baptist Church." If anyone had seen the spot where the church was built, he would know why this name was chosen.

Within the year, our neighbors who belonged to the other neighborhood church, the Methodist church, decided that they also needed a new church. Their building committee was headed up by Kelley Caswell. He was a very popular person, especially with the young men of the neighborhood. He formed clubs for us and took us fishing and camping at places where we had never been.

The Baptist church was brick. The Methodists decided to build their church with mountain stone. The stone was free for the hauling out of the pastures on the side of little Sam Mountain. Kelley had a large truck that he donated for the rock hauling. He called for volunteers to do the collecting and hauling. He had no trouble getting all the help he needed from both the Methodists and Baptists, and he began hauling rocks from the Mountain. Soon he had a large pile of stone in the field near where the new church was to be built.

Digging the basement wasn't too much of a job. There were no trees to be removed as there were at Oak Grove. Masons and carpenters were hired, and the building was on its way. I worked some on this church, too. I mixed cement for the rock masons, and they paid me the usual ten cents an hour.

This new church would be called "Rockwood Methodist Church." We now had two new churches in our area, but things didn't change in our neighborhood. We were still neighbors. When one of our two churches planned a program, it planned it so that it would not conflict with a program at the other church. The Baptists would attend the Methodist church for their programs, and the Methodists would attend the Baptist church for their programs. Again, we were neighbors.

I have my doubts that anything similar to what we did would ever happen in these so-called modern times. In those days, if any of our neighbors was behind in gathering his crops because of sickness or any other unforeseen problem, his neighbors—whether they be Baptist or Methodist, Republican or Democrat, or whatever—always came to his rescue. Wouldn't it be wonderful if things were like that in this day and time? We now live closer to each other. We have telephones, newspapers, televisions, cars, and other ways to communicate with each other, but do all of us use these means of communication to get to know the ones who live in our neighborhoods as neighbors? I'm afraid not. We live near each other, but are we really neighbors?

# DIGGING THE WELL

The thing that led to the digging of the well can partially be blamed on the New Deal. That was the group of programs started by Franklin D. Roosevelt, our president who went into office during the darkest days of our country's history. He started many programs to give jobs to anyone that wanted to work. One of these programs was the Work Projects Administration (WPA). The WPA had many projects. One was to repair roads and build new roads throughout the mountains of North Carolina. One of these roads was built through the property of "Uncle George" Wines.

The original route of the old Thickety Road was east of the Uncle George's blacksmith shop. There was no bridge over the creek there. To get across you had to ford the creek. The route for the new road would be between Uncle George's house and his spring house. This would eliminate fording the spring branch or building a bridge and keep the new road on dry ground. But it also caused a problem. The Wines family had to cross the new road in order to get to their spring house.

This bothered Uncle George an awful lot. All of the Wines' water came from the spring across the new road. Uncle George was always worrying that someone would get run over by a car while crossing the road with a bucket of water. So, Uncle George came up with a plan to keep from crossing the road: Dig a well.

He came up with another idea, too: the well should be under the house. This would save the cost of building a well house and also avoid having to go outside in bad weather. He didn't think about there not being any stairs from inside the house to the basement.

Like everyone else, he didn't have any money to pay a professional well digger to do the job. The job of digging the well was given to guess who?—his youngest son, Conrad, who was very large for a sixteen-year-old. Anyone knows that one person can't dig a well by himself, so guess who Conrad asked for help?—me, his best friend, who was young and didn't know what he was getting into.

First we had to lay out the diameter of the well, so we used some string attached to a stick pounded into the ground as our compass and made a perfect circle. We began digging, and it wasn't too long until we were about four feet deep. Then we hit solid mountain rock. We went to the blacksmith shop for a sledge hammer and started hitting the rock with it.—Bam! Wham! Bang!—But the only thing we accomplished was to make sparks fly from the rock.

Conrad rolled himself a cigarette from his sack of "Golden Grain," struck a match, lit up, and went into deep thought. He threw the cigarette down, put his foot on it and said, "Let's go."

"Where?" I asked.

"To the barn," he replied.

"Why?" I asked.

"To get the horses," he replied.

"Why?" I said.

"I've got this thing all worked out," he said. "Just follow me."

We bridled up two of Uncle George's horses and off we went. I quit asking what he had in mind because he wasn't about to tell me. It so happened that some mining company was mining kaolin, (a mineral used for making chinaware) up on Little Sam Mountain. I soon figured out the mine was our destination. *But why there?* I thought. I soon found out.

After about an hour's ride we were at the kaolin mine. Conrad talked to the miners, and he soon had two sticks of dynamite, ten foot of fuse, and dynamite caps. Then down Little Sam we went heading to Uncle George's house and our well.

After putting the horses back in the pasture, we went to the blacksmith shop and got steel bits to drill with and another large hammer. Back at the well site I held the steel bits while Conrad did the hammering. After about two hours, we had a hole in the center of the rock about six inches deep and two inches wide. By this time I knew what was to take place: we were going to bust that rock with dynamite.

Conrad said, "I can't get these two sticks of dynamite in this hole, so I'll lay one on top of the rock."

"Don't you think we should tell your dad what we are doing?" I said.

"Naw. He might stop us, and I've got a whole dollar tied up in this blasting stuff."

"Let's try a half stick first," I said.

"No. It'll take all of the two sticks to do the job," he argued.

It wasn't easy, but I finally convinced him to try only a half-stick. We put the half stick of dynamite into the hole, installed the blasting cap, and put the fuse in place. Next, we carried in about twenty wooden fence posts to cover the top of the well so the rock wouldn't hit the floor of the house above the well.

It was the fall of the year and cool outside. Above in the house, the family were sitting around a wood-burning stove keeping warm—all but "Aunt Seet." Aunt Seet was about 50 years old and had never married. She had been sick for several years, and was in bed most of the time.

Below the house, Conrad lit the fuse with a match, and out we ran from under the house. It seemed like hours, but finally the dynamite exploded—B-O-O-M! The fence posts hit the underside of the floor, the whole house shook, and Aunt Seet ran out the back door screaming, "Lord, the end of time has come!"

Someone got Aunt Seet back in the house to keep her from freezing while Uncle George came toward the basement. He had Conrad and me trapped in the basement where we were inspecting the results of our blasting. He grabbed Conrad, but I escaped through the smoke and headed for home, hearing Uncle George scream, "I'm putting the both of you in jail! The world's not safe with you two running around!"

Conrad broke loose and headed for the woods. I didn't go back to the Wines' house for quite some time after that. After everyone settled down and things got back to normal, Uncle George hired a well-digging crew, but he wouldn't let them dig any closer to the house than 200 feet.

In a few weeks the Wines family didn't have to cross the new road to get their water. Uncle George was happy, and no one was killed by a car. The well digging was finished. Conrad and I were soon back together. Uncle George had forgotten about the dynamite.

# AN AIRPLANE RIDE

The marvels of the future were beginning to appear daily in the 1930s, one of these being the airplane. Every so often a small plane would land in someone's cow pasture and offer rides to anyone that had a dollar. There were more spectators than riders, all gawking and "ohs" "ahs" when the pilot did flips and spins. Some shut their eyes to keep from seeing these maneuvers. Well, little did I know that I would soon take my first airplane ride.

It was in the winter of 1935. That winter we had one of the biggest snow storms that western North Carolina had ever seen. Not only was there snow, but the temperature was below zero for several days. About a week after the storm, it began to warm up, and every thing was getting back to normal. Our nearest neighbor, Carroll Clark, found two of his largest steers dead. They had not been able to get to the barn during the storm and had frozen to death. There wasn't any machinery to dig graves for them, so his plans were to drag the carcasses up to the foot of the mountain and let the buzzards eat them.

It so happened that Carroll's brother-in-law, Bill Cordell, came by and viewed the problem of moving the dead cattle.

"Say. Why don't we skin 'em and sell the hides to the Swift Packing House in Asheville? They buy cow hides," he said to me.

"How much do you think we'd get for them?" I asked.

"At least five or six dollars," Bill said.

Bill was about eighteen years old—three years older than me. He also owned his own car. I guess this had something to do with him and me being good friends. I had to walk, otherwise.

Well, we started the skinning job. It wasn't easy. The steer carcasses were frozen stiff. This made the job of skinning harder than usual. It took the better part of a day to skin the two steers, but we didn't give up.

About three or four days later, the snow had all melted, and the weather warmed up. Bill decided that it was time to take the skins to Asheville and make some money. So, off we went to the packing house. We were on our way to becoming rich. We sold the two hides for five dollars: $2.50 for Bill and $2.50 for me. We were wealthy.

Bill said, "Now that we have some money, let's go out to the airport and take an airplane ride."

"Sounds good to me," I said.

So, off we went. We found one of the pilots and asked about the ride and the cost.

"Well, things are pretty slow, and I need to warm up my plane, so I'll give you two a ride for two dollars—one dollar each. Load up," he told us.

Within ten minutes everything on the ground looked real small. I was holding onto the seat really tight and was a little scared. "Do you boys want me to do a few loops?" the pilot asked.

"No!" we said. "Take us back down. We've had our money's worth."

It was many years later before I took another airplane ride, and it was on a larger plane.

# MODEL A FORD

I was sixteen years old now and had a good job. I was working for the National Youth Administration (NYA). This was another program of President Roosevelt's New Deal. The purpose of the program was to give young men a chance to learn a trade and at the same time earn some money.

Our work included many projects. We cleaned off graveyards that had been neglected for many years. We built football fields complete with stadiums. They were made of mountain stone. Some are being used today. There was plenty of stone on the mountainsides, so material didn't cost anything.

The largest project I worked on was a garage for state-owned school buses. It was located in Waynesville and was also made from stone. All the work was supervised by qualified stone masons. Our work schedule was two weeks of work at 40 hours a week and two weeks off. The pay was thirty cents an hour. This was the highest pay I had ever received.

The job in Waynesville created a problem for me. It was over twelve miles away from where I was living. It was impossible for me to walk that distance and be on time to go to work, so someone from our area had to buy a car. I was in town one Saturday (as I was every Saturday). I went to Mr. King's used car lot. Mr. King was the husband of my former school teacher at Beaverdam. I was looking around the car lot, and Mr. King came out and asked if he could help me.

"I'm looking for a car," I said. "What is the cheapest one you have?"

He pointed to a Ford Model A touring car. It was black with no curtains and bad tires, but it had a good cloth top, the paint was good, and there weren't any dents or scratch marks on it. To me it was a beauty.

"How much?" I asked.

"Sixty dollars," he said.

"Sure a lot of money," I said. "I'll think it over. I may come back after a while."

After the usual Saturday movie—a western and a Popeye cartoon—I went back to the car lot to see if the Ford was still there. It was. So was Mr. King.

"I can't get that much money today," I told Mr. King.

He looked me over pretty well and said, "I know money is scarce, and young men your age don't get very much work. I'll tell you what I'll do. If you can get forty-five dollars today, I'll let you have the car for that much."

I already had thirty dollars from my NYA pay, so off I went looking for fifteen dollars. I found my brother, TJ, and told him I needed forty-five dollars, and I had only thirty. I told him if he would lend me fifteen dollars, I could buy a car, and I'd pay him back when I got my next pay, and I'd teach him how to drive. He told me he'd let me have the loan. Whoopee! My problem was solved.

I went back to the car lot and bought the car. By the time Mr. King had made out the bill of sale and had put enough gas in the tank to get me home, it was well after dark. I was afraid to drive through town although there wasn't any traffic. The road home was paved to the edge of town at the Fiberville Bridge. I started looking for someone to drive the car to the bridge for me. I found my friend Bill Cordell, my partner on the airplane ride. I explained my problem to him, and he said he would help me. He drove the car to the Fiberville Bridge.

Off we went around the Pigeon River Road. Only about three miles, and I would be home to show off my prize possession. It took me quite a while to make those three miles. Steering the car was hard for me. Cars didn't have any power steering back then. They only had mechanical steering. You had to turn the steering wheel nearly all the way around before it would turn the front wheels.

I finally arrived at the cattle gate that was across the road that led to our house. The road was on the side of a steep hill and only wide enough for one car to travel it. Well, I chickened out. I was afraid to try to drive on that narrow road, and I wasn't about to leave my car sitting on the main road.

It was about one A.M. by then. Everyone was in bed asleep. I had no choice but to walk to the house and get my dad to drive the car to the house. I woke him and explained the problem. He got out of bed, put on his clothes, and went to get the car. The commotion had everyone awake by now. I was excited. "I'll drive and take you all to church tomorrow morning," I told everyone. Finally everyone settled back into bed for a few more hours of sleep.

Sunday morning I got up bright and early ready to take my mother, sisters, and brother to church. Everyone got into the car but Mom. "I'll walk," she said. "It's not too far, and the walk will be good for me." I could see that she was afraid of my driving, so I didn't beg her to ride.

Now I was ready to haul passengers to and from the NYA job in Waynesville. I had room for five passengers. By the following Monday, which was the start of the two-week work period, I had a full car load of people: four boys and one girl. (There was a female section of the NYA—I don't know what they did. I let the girl out at a building in Waynesville.) I charged each person twenty cents a day for the ride to work and back. This earned me five dollars a week for gas and other expenses to keep the Ford running.

This car never had good breaks or tires as long as I owned it. The brakes were mechanical and needed new linings. The tires all had one or more boots (patches) in them, and the bladders (inner tubes) were covered with patches. I didn't have the money to fix either of these problems.

One afternoon we were on our way home from work on old Highway 19 / 23 near a roadhouse called Little Rock. There weren't many tourists back then, but it happened that one was going to stop at Little Rock just as we came by. He stopped, but I couldn't. My car didn't have any brakes, so I ran directly into the rear end of the tourist's car. No one was hurt, and there was no damage to either car. I apologized to the tourist, we shook hands, and we were on our way again.

I kept the car for about a year and sold it for forty-five dollars. I had plans to go into the Civilian Conservation Corps (CCC). But I also need the money. I sure hated to part with that Ford.

You know what? I never did teach TJ to drive.

## CHARLES C. FLETCHER

# CCC CAMP

My uncle Clifford (my mother's youngest brother) and I had discussed the possibility of going into the Civilian Conservation Corps (CCC) camps. This also was one of the New Deal projects started by President Roosevelt. There were around 1300 camps around the country, several being in the Great Smokey Mountains. The camps were set up to provide jobs for thousands of unemployed young men. Men between the ages of 17 and 25 who were unmarried, out of school, and unemployed were eligible. The pay was $30.00 a month. The men got $5.00, and $25.00 was sent home to their families. If a person had no family, the money was held in an account until his discharge from the CCC.

The CCC hired local experienced men to teach the camp crews how to do the jobs they were assigned to do. Each camp also had Army officers responsible for day-to-day operations. All the men were given clothing, shelter, and food in addition to their pay. At this time, the Army was feeding their men for 45¢ a day. The CCC men were allowed $1.50 a day for food. We got three good meals every day.

The work of the CCCs was a variety of jobs. They built telephone lines, roads, and bridges, planted trees, fought forest fires, stocked streams with fish, cut stone for walls, ran nurseries to grow tree seedlings, and did many other things. They had instructors to teach trades to anyone that wanted to learn a trade.

Clifford and I hitched a ride on a slow freight train to Waynesville from Canton. We went to the county courthouse to sign up for the CCC. We were given a date for the next selection of enrollees. We were to be at the courthouse no later than eight A.M. on the appointed day to leave for camp. About thirty of us got into the back of an Army truck and set off. None of the enrollees knew where we were going.

About two hours later we were unloading at a camp in Round Bottoms near the Cherokee Indian reservation. I believe the camp was called Ravensford. They fed us a very good lunch. Most of us had never seen so much food and so many different kinds of it. After lunch they began the process of choosing the men they wanted to keep. They only had room for twenty new people. Uncle Clifford was a big stout boy. I weighed maybe one-hundred pounds. They kept Clifford and sent me back to Waynesville along with nine others. We were promised that we would be on the next month's list. I sure was let down. I wanted to be with my uncle.

I reported for the next month's trip. Again, we were told only that we were going to a CCC camp but not where. After a pretty long ride the truck stopped, and we were told to get out. None of us recognized the place. We were told that the camp number was 411 and that the place was Smokemont (the Kephart Camp). They kept all of us as enrollees. They explained the rules that we were to follow. They told us we were not to get any clothing until we had stayed one week. At that time khaki uniforms would be issued to us. Then they assigned us to a barrack like building.

On Monday morning right after breakfast everyone gathered at the Park Office for work assignments. All work assignments were given by Forest Service personnel. I was to go with the rock cutting crew. Our workplace was at a location along Highway 411 near a rock quarry.

The supervisor would have a large piece of rock placed on a table. He took a rule and did some measuring, made lines on the rock with a piece of chalk, and then said something like, "I want this stone to be x inches long and y inches wide and z inches deep with all sides as smooth as you can make them." He then handed me a large hammer and a couple of chisels, telling me, "When the chisels get dull, holler and someone will bring you some sharp ones."

There I was, in the hot sun, wearing a blue denim shirt and pants. I did not have a hat. I was wearing all the clothes that I owned. Sweat was pouring off this one-hundred pound boy. I had cut places on my arms and face, and I was working hard trying to show them I could take it. I was glad when that day was over. I was tired, sore, and hungry. The hungry part was soon gone because we had a very good supper. I took a good shower and went straight to bed.

This kept up for the whole week. I was getting more cuts and bruises. Also, my only clothes were dirty and beginning to get holes in them. I made myself a promise: come Saturday, (no work on Saturday or Sunday) I was going "over the hill" (going home) and not coming back. Saturday morning I got up at five while everyone in the barracks was asleep and headed down the mile long road to Highway 411 going toward Cherokee.

One of the rules of the camp was never to hitchhike or beg a ride from anyone. I was walking down Highway 411 long before daylight, when out of nowhere came a green pickup truck. I stuck out my thumb. I was desperate. I had to get out of those mountains. At that time there were lots of wild animals in the mountains. The truck stopped. It was still dark, and I didn't see who was giving me a ride.

"What are you doing up here in these mountains at this time of the day?" the driver asked.

"Well, I was in that CCC camp up there, but I'm going home, and I ain't coming back."

"What's the problem?" he asked.

"I can't take that rock quarry. Look at the cuts and bruises on my face and arms. Lots of dust got in my eyes. We didn't have goggles. I don't mind working long, hard days, but I can't take that quarry."

It was getting light now, and I saw that the man who was driving was wearing green clothes. This bothered me. I knew that he belonged to the US Forest Service. He said, "Son, my name is J.O. Rosser. I'm the park superintendent from headquarters at Gatlinburg. If you will come back on Sunday and report for duty, I promise you that you will never go back to the rock pit again. What do you say?"

"I don't know. I'll have to think it over," I said.

We talked about other things until we were at Waynesville. "This is as far as I go," he said. "I'm going to a fire camp up at Catalooch. See you Monday."

"Maybe," I said.

I had to walk from Waynesville to Canton because there weren't many cars on the road, especially on Saturday. There wasn't much to do around home that weekend. Everyone seemed to have something to do except me. Come Sunday noon, I decided to go back to camp. I had pride; I wasn't a quitter; I'd show them.

I got a ticket and boarded the Trailways bus that went to Knoxville by way of Gatlinburg. The bus stopped on 411 where the road to the CCC camp was. I made it in time for supper. I never got food this good at home. This was one of the things that brought me back.

Monday morning I reported to the park office where all the work assignments were given out. Everyone had left for work but me. I stood there, and the Park Supervisor motioned for me. I went to him, and he said, "Son, from now on your job will be to help out in the Park Office. You'll issue tools and keep records of who gets gas and how much they get and also have them sign for the gas." He knew my name. I guess Mr. Rosser told him because he had asked me my name on our ride to Waynesville on Saturday.

One of the perks of this job was that I moved into the Office bedroom. The reason for this is that I would have to answer the phone if any fires or emergencies were reported and make contact with the ones who needed to know about them. I shared this duty with the Park Clerk who also had to be on duty 24 hours each day. During the day when nothing was going on, I would practice driving the road graders and army trucks that were at the camp. Things were not so bad after all. I'm glad I went back.

Our company was run by two Army officers, a captain by the name of Miller and a 1st lieutenant whose name I've forgotten. Everyone liked the captain because he was like one of us. He didn't try to push us too far. This wasn't true with the Louie. He was sort of a smart-aleck who liked to show his authority.

As with most CCC camps there were many mountain boys who would only take so much pushing and then they would do some getting even. This happened to the Lieutenant several times. As in the Army, we had to "sack our beds," so the officers' beds were sacked also. One night after lights out, there was a scream from the officers' quarters. It was the Louie. Somehow, a great big black snake had found a sleeping place between the tightly stretched sheets on his bed. He called a meeting, but no one knew anything about that snake, and besides, everyone claimed to be scared to death of any kind of snake. Everyone went back to bed with a grin on his face—that is, except the Lieutenant.

Another time, when all the workers came to camp for dinner (lunch), they left the Mess Hall and all sat down on the rock wall in front of the barracks instead of reporting to the Park Office to be taken back to work. The officers were called; they had us all go to the Recreation Hall. The captain wanted to know what the problem was. The spokesman for the CCC boys told the captain that there wouldn't be anymore work until the food got better. It was the duty of the Lieutenant to purchase all supplies. He bought all the food locally in Bryson City or Sylva and had been buying cheap meat and vegetables.

The captain said he would personally promise that the food would be better. He then asked, "Is there anyone here who's hungry?"

A boy by the name of Forgy spoke up. "I am," he said.

Now, old Forgy was an over-sized mountain boy who was our Fire Watch and took care of the generators that supplied our electric power for lighting. The cooks had joined the meeting, also. The captain whispered something to the Head Cook, and he left. He soon returned with a large box of soda crackers (saltines) and a gallon tin can of Vienna sausages. The captain told the Cook to give this to Forgy. He took both the crackers and sausages, sat down at a table and began eating. Everyone left to go back to work except Forgy. When the last one left, Forgy was still eating his crackers and sausages.

My friend Forgy met with the captain again later on. As mentioned, he was Fire Watch, so his job was at night. He usually slept pretty much in the day time. He also could go to the Mess Hall whenever he wanted to eat, and the cooks would feed him.

One day while at the mess hall eating, he heard a lot of noise out back of the Mess Hall. He went to find out what was going on. There were several black bears eating out of the garbage cans. One of the smaller bears was inside of an overturned can. Forgy took the lid of the can and shoved the bear inside, put the lid on the can, turned it up, and sat on the top.

"Go get the captain! Go get the captain!" Forgy hollered.

Someone told the captain that Forgy needed to see him out behind the mess hall. The captain walked out back and saw Forgy sitting on top of the garbage can.

"What do you want?" he asked.

"Cap, I've got a bear in this can. Take your gun and shoot through the side and kill him. I'll skin him, and the cooks will cook him, and we'll have bear for dinner tomorrow."

"Get off that can and let that bear go," ordered the captain.

"But bear meat is really good eating, and I ain't had any since I left home," Forgy complained.

"Git," said the captain.

Forgy got off the can slowly, and the bear jumped out and headed for higher ground. Forgy returned to his eating. The captain headed back to his quarters with a smile on his face wondering if there would be other meetings with his friend Forgy, the fire watchman.

As I mentioned, everyone liked the captain. He had a small radio with about 100 feet of aerial that would let him get a station from St. Louis where the Cardinals baseball team was. He let us listen to the broadcast of the ballgames. We were all Cardinals fans.

Saturday was the day most everyone looked forward to. First thing was that there was no working, with the exception of necessary work such as that of the cooks, the Vehicle Checker (who checked cars entering and leaving the Smokies), and a few others. Everyone else piled into the back of a truck and headed to the towns of Bryson City or Sylva for a recreation trip. We could see a movie if we had the dime for a ticket. Then there was the most important event, the Saturday night square dance. Even if you didn't dance, you always met a lot of pretty country girls. They, too, came out on Saturday for the same reason that the CCC boys did. They wanted to meet the CCC boys. Everybody was happy. Some of the older boys fell in love (so they said) and later married the girls they met.

One Saturday night I was taking my girl friend home. I asked her how far away she lived because the truck back to camp left at 11 P.M., and if you weren't in the truck, they didn't wait for you. She told me it wasn't very far. So, off we went hand in hand, across foot logs, through the woods, and over fences.

I didn't have a watch, but something told me I had better head back to town, or I would be walking the 30-plus miles back to camp. I said a quick goodbye, and here I went, running as fast as I could in the dark. I soon saw the lights of town, and I thought if I was lucky I would make it. I just did get there in time. I was the last one getting on the truck. This was the last time I offered to take my dancing partner home.

We didn't spend much money on these trips, maybe a few nickels for soft drinks. We didn't have much money. Our five dollars a month pay didn't last very long. Most of it was spent in the Canteen at camp for cigarettes and chewing tobacco.

I began to get a real education while in the CCCs. I learned how to take care of myself and how to get along with other people even though none of us ever thought alike. There were as many personalities as there were people. Even with our different ways of thinking, we were like a family. Everyone helped, and we looked out for each other. As I write this I keep thinking how things have changed since the days I was in the CCCs. We were poor in worldly possessions but rich in the way we treated each other. In other words, we were humble because we were all alike—we were all poor people.

# VIRGINIA

I was still in the CCC camp when the Japanese bombed Pearl Harbor. I remember when it happened really well. It was on a weekend. I was at my girlfriend's house. Her family had a radio. We were listening, and the program was interrupted by the news of how the Japanese slipped in and sank nearly all of the American ships in port at Pearl Harbor, Hawaii.

I returned to camp, and everyone was talking about either joining the service or getting a defense job. I wasn't old enough to join the service, so I decided to look for a defense job. I had heard that there was plenty of work in the shipyards at Norfolk or Newport News, Virginia. Also, I knew a boy who I went to school with who was working in the shipyards at Newport News. I contacted his parents to get his address, and they gave it to me.

Also, I had been told that there was a boom in the housing business. The government was having houses built for the families who were left behind when the man of the home was sent off to war. This was many thousands of men. The word was, if you could drive a nail and use a hand saw, you could get a job as a carpenter that paid big money—75¢ to $1.00 an hour. I spent a little of the money I had saved for a cheap hand saw and a claw hammer. I was going prepared to be a first-class carpenter.

I made arrangements at camp to take a leave of absence to check out the jobs. If I should get a defense job, I was to notify the commander at camp, and I would be honorably discharged, and any money that I was due would be mailed to me.

On the next Saturday I purchased a ticket for a ride to Newport News, Virginia. I boarded the Trailways bus about four in the evening.

I had my saw and hammer and nothing else. I had no extra clothes to take. Around midnight the bus stopped for a break so the passengers could stretch their legs. I got my ticket out of my pocket and saw that somehow or someway I had messed up. The ticket was for Norfolk instead of Newport News where my friend was.

My friend in Newport News was going to let me stay with him until I could find a place of my own. What was I to do? I only had $1.00 left after buying the bus ticket. But there was no turning back. I told myself not to be afraid. Although I tried to tell myself to have faith that I would find something, it wasn't easy for seventeen (nearly eighteen) year old boy 300 miles from home. I didn't know anyone in Norfolk. I didn't have any food or any place to sleep, and I had only $1.00 in my pocket.

The bus arrived in Norfolk a little after one P.M. on Sunday evening. I got off and looked around trying to decide which way to go. I walked around town looking for a YMCA or some other place that would let me sleep that night. I never found one. I did see a hotel that had a sign outside advertising "Sleeping Rooms // Men Only // $1.00 a Night." I was hungry. I hadn't eaten anything since leaving home on Saturday. I also needed a place to sleep. I had to make a choice. I decided that I had better invest in the dollar room. I needed rest for the next day's job hunting.

My saw, my hammer, and I moved into a room on the third floor. It was a small room, and I noticed there were two beds in the room. I didn't undress. I put the saw and hammer under one of the beds and climbed into bed fully clothed (except for my shoes). I was very tired, and I fell asleep right away.

The next morning I was in for a surprise. In the other bed was a giant of a man with a beardy face and not very clean or neat. Although I was afraid, I broke the ice trying to be friendly by saying, "Looks like it's going to be a nice day." The man said something in another language. He talked some more, but I didn't understand, and I got my shoes on and got out of there.

I headed for the shipyards. The first dock I came to hired me. I had to start immediately if I wanted the job. I said, "I'm ready to go to work." They gave me something that they called an "air chipping hammer." They then had me sit on a board that they called a "scaffold." I wasn't alone; there were men every four feet along the scaffolding, and they also had hammers like mine. We were raised up to the top of a pretty large ship. The men turned a handle they called a "valve," and their hammers began vibrating. They then began knocking round rock-like things off the ship's side until you could see the metal underneath. They called these rock-like things "barnacles." I did like they did; acting like I knew what was going on. I didn't know what was going on or what I was doing, but the others didn't know that.

The sun was bearing down on us, and the reflection from the ship's side made it very hot. We never came down until a whistle was blown at the twelve o'clock dinner time—that is, dinner time for the others but not for me. I started looking for a place to board.

Not far from the shipyard I saw a vacancy sign on the porch of a large house. I went to the door and knocked, and a lady came to the door. I asked about the room, and she said that it was twelve dollars a week paid in advance. This included two meals and a packed lunch. I explained my situation: that I didn't have any money but was working.

"Where are you from?" she asked.

"North Carolina. Canton," I said.

"Well," (she was looking me over) "it so happens that my husband and I are from North Carolina. Been up here nearly ten years. I'm going to take a chance on you for one week. All the people who I've had dealings with who were from North Carolina were honest. Supper is at six. Wash up before you come to the table."

I went back to work. Time went by very slowly. I was thinking about six o'clock. I sure was hungry. At supper I was ashamed of myself the way I ate. I like to never stopped. And it was a good meal: meat and lots of vegetables. Her husband had a farm to grow all the vegetables and also had hogs that he killed to feed the boarders.

I worked at the barnacle chipping job the rest of that week. I had found another job that paid more at Woods Dry Dock Company. I was to report to work on Monday morning. So, I informed my supervisor that I was quitting on Friday. He paid me for that week's work. I had enough money for my room and board and enough to pay for a week in advance. I was on my way to being wealthy.

The job at Woods Dry Dock lasted for one week. After a few days they had me and another fellow get inside a large tank on a ship. We were to paint the inside. There wasn't any ventilation in the tank, and the paint fumes were making us sleepy. The worker who was with me was older and crawled out through the small opening on the tank. I became so sleepy that I just got out in time before passing out.

I went to the office and asked the supervisor if he had another job for me. He said that someone had to do the painting. I said, "It won't be me." He did some figuring on a paper pad and handed a note to me to take to the office up town in order to pick up the pay for the work that I had done that week. I got my pay and went to the boarding house.

I had made friends with two brothers who were living at the house. They worked for a heating company that installed oil furnaces in the houses that were being built for the families left behind by sailors sent to sea. The company was owned by an ex-boxer. He was married to the mayor's daughter. This helped him get all the work he wanted. The brothers were from North Carolina. They said that the company they worked for needed another worker. They spoke to their boss, and he told them to bring me to work on Sunday. They had so much work that they had to work lots of weekends. I went for a tryout, and Mr. Hunley said I had a full-time job if I wanted to stay. I stayed. The pay was good, and the working conditions were the best you could ask for.

Every chance we had to get away for a night, Mr. Hunley would treat all of the installers to a steak dinner, a burlesque show, or a wrestling match, whichever the majority wanted. He would also go with us sometimes. I believe he used this as an excuse to get away from home. He was a great fellow to work for. He also let us keep the service cars or trucks for our personal use when we were not on duty.

He wanted the brothers and me to live closer to him so we could catch service calls at night. He had asked a friend who lived close by to make two bedrooms upstairs in his house and let us board with his family. They were a very nice family. They had three little girls. The lady of the house liked a beer once in a while, but the husband would never drink. They both were good sports and liked lots of fun.

They had plans for a young boy named James Trull and me. James was only eighteen. I was nearing twenty. He, too, was from North Carolina. One night after supper the wife wanted James and me to go with her somewhere. She didn't tell us where. We went to a house that had a ladies' beauty shop downstairs and living quarters upstairs. She introduced us to the lady who lived there. They sent James and me out to buy some beer. We did this, and when we returned, they kept getting us to drink with them. Being young and not drinkers, we soon became pretty high. We went home some time that night; I don't know what time it was.

When we awoke the next morning and were washing up, I looked in the mirror and saw that my hair was kinky—curly. Also, my head had burns on it. I looked at James, and he was the same. We had been given a free permanent wave. James was pleased or didn't care. Me, I rubbed grease on my hair to try to get rid of the curly hair, but the curl wouldn't go away. I bought me a cap and wore it all the time that I wasn't in bed. Everyone thought it was funny but me. Finally, my hair grew straight again.

Once I had my twentieth birthday, here came the "Greetings" letter. I was directed to register for induction into the armed services. The draft age had been lowered from twenty-one to twenty. I went to Suffolk, Virginia, and registered. A week later I received another greetings message. This, I knew, was it. I was on my way into the armed services. I wouldn't open the letter. I had the lady I boarded with note on the envelope that I had returned to North Carolina. Next, I called the boss and had him come over. I told him that it was very important. He came over right soon.

I handed him the keys for the Plymouth station wagon that I used for work, saying "I'm going home to be drafted."

"You don't have to be drafted," he said. "The work we do is classed as a defense job. I can keep you out of the Army."

"No," I said. "I'm going home so I will be with boys I grew up with."

He said, "I won't give you your pay."

"That's okay," I said. "Jim is taking me to the bus station now."

He paid me despite what he said and told me if I made it thru the war to come back, and I would always have a job. I left Virginia a lot more grown-up man.

## CHARLES C. FLETCHER

# DRAFTED

Bill had given me the pay that he owed me for the last week of work, and James Trull took me to the Trailways bus station. I was on my way back to North Carolina. It was late in the evening before my bus left Norfolk. The trip on the way back to Carolina was a lot different from the bus ride I took when going to Virginia. This time I had money to get a cup of coffee or a sandwich when the bus stopped for a stretch break.

It was in the evening the following day that I arrived in Canton. No one was expecting me because I hadn't had time to write a letter. I couldn't call because Mom and Dad didn't have a telephone. In fact, no one had phones outside town. Our mode of communication was to send a runner to the person you had a message for. Your neighbor in the mountains was usually a mile or more from where you lived. Anyway, my family was glad to see me, but they wondered why I had made the sudden trip home. I explained the reason for coming home: I wanted to go into the Army from Canton instead of leaving for service from Virginia because I wanted to go with boys I had known all my life.

It happened, and lots quicker than I thought it would. I soon received the letter from our president with an invitation to be a part of the US Army. It didn't bother me at all. In a way I was honored. After all, most young men in our community had already left for service. So I was ready to report to the local draft board immediately. They would take care of everything after that.

I reported the next morning. They gave me some forms to fill out. Then I was told what day and time to be at the bus station. I was to be there at eight A.M. the next Monday. I didn't need to bring anything because this was a one-day trip.

I was at the station bright and early on Monday morning. There were about ten other men there. I knew a few of them. The bus arrived at exactly eight o'clock. A man from the draft board called our names, we got on the bus, and off we went.

The bus stopped in Asheville, and another ten or fifteen men got on the bus. We made two more stops, and we had a busload of future soldiers. The next stop was Camp Croft, an Army base in South Carolina.

We unloaded and were given an early lunch. We then went into a large building that I later learned was a hospital or, in this case, an examination room. We were naked for the rest of that day. We went from doctor to doctor. Some were looking up, some were looking down. We were given lots of commands: bend over; stretch out your arms; make a fist; stick out your tongue; stand on one foot. There was no end to the things they wanted to look at.

I think they finally got tired. They lined us up (still nude) and marched us into another room. Men in white coats with long needles in their hands formed two lines, one on each side of us. I think they were a team of left-handed stickers and right-handed stickers—sort of like left-handed and right-handed pitchers on a baseball team. They began to give us shots.

Finally, they were through and told us that we could put our clothes back on. I was glad. I had started to get cold running around bare. I felt sort of like I usually did when we went skinny dipping in the winter time.

Once clothed, we were taken into another room. We lined up in rows of ten. There were lots of rows because our bus load was not the only one. Enlistees had come from all directions. We were told to raise our right hands and to repeat what a captain said. This was our oath.

After we had repeated the things the captain said, he told us that we were no longer civilians, that we were now soldiers in the United

States Army, and that each of us would get further instructions. They handed each of us an envelope as we marched out, telling us that these were our orders. My group boarded a bus to return to Canton.

Once we were on the bus and on our way, I opened my envelope to see what was next. My orders said that I was to report to the bus station the next Monday morning at eight A.M. The orders also listed what to bring with me. It wasn't much—a little money, a razor, and toothbrush. We had one whole week to take care of any business that needed taking care of. This didn't bother me. I didn't have anything to take care of. I spent that week saying goodbye to all of my friends, male and female, asking them to write to me sometimes (especially the girls).

I sure would miss the square dances that we had pretty often at Arthur Ford's barn. He had hardwood flooring put in the loft of his barn just for dancing. I and the ones who went to the dances were frowned on by some of the neighbors. They said it was "the devil's work." I went to the dances often, and I never saw anything that was vulgar, nor did I ever see a drunken man or anyone fighting. It was just good, clean fun.

The week went by fast. We were to meet at the bus station the same as the week before. Not all the men who went the last time reported. Some were to take another bus. They were going somewhere other than where we were going. Some others were picked up along the way until we had a full load. Our first stop was in Charlotte, North Carolina. We were to have lunch in a hotel there, and the Army was paying for it.

I saw one of the strangest things I had ever seen at that hotel. It was a new building with all the modern things of that time, 1942. As we entered the lobby, the large glass door opened by itself. All the others went through except me. I backed off and went forward. The door opened again without anyone pushing it. I finally went inside and to the dining room to eat my lunch. Being a curious person, I asked one of the employees at the hotel about the door. He explained to me how it worked.

I had no idea where we were going, but late that afternoon we pulled into a camp called Fort Bragg. This camp was in North Carolina. We had a welcoming committee: a couple of tough-looking sergeants and two corporals. After a cool welcome, we were lined up and marched to the post barber shop. The barbers would ask how you would like your hair to be cut, but regardless of what you told them, they gave everyone the same style—clipped down to the skin. "That will be a quarter, please," the barber would then say. You weren't in the chair more than two minutes.

Next, we were marched to the Supply Room. Here again, they would ask you your size of pants and shirts, but if you told them it was a 30" waist and a 32" leg length, they gave you pants with a 32" waist and a 34" leg length. We also got underwear, sheets, blankets, socks, handkerchiefs, a razor, shaving soap, a shaving brush, a toothbrush, toothpaste, hand soap, washcloths, towels, a helmet, a 30.06 rifle, a web belt, a first aid kit, a gas mask (that we were never to be caught without), boots (that were too large), and a duffel bag.

For most things, we were issued two of everything. I had never had this many worldly goods in my whole life. I felt sort of proud to have all these things, but I could barely carry such a load. I hadn't grown up to be strong enough to handle this heavy a load.

After going through Supply, we were marched to a two-story barrack and assigned bunks. I got the top floor. We were told we would live here for the next three months. We were told to keep our "home" clean and neat or else suffer the consequences. The sergeant in charge told us, "You belong to Battery D, 7th Battalion, 3rd Regiment of the Field Artillery Training Center. Your commanding officer is Captain Pugh, and I am your Platoon Sergeant. Any questions?"

The next three months were sort of hectic. We went through KP, guard duty, forced marches, the obstacle course, the rifle range, aircraft shooting, bayonet drill, hand-to-hand combat, and lots of other things to make sure we stayed busy. We also had to practice boarding and de-boarding a troop ship. Looking back, it wasn't all that hard on us. When we finished, we were pretty well prepared considering the short time of the 90-day training. They fed us well, took care of our health, and taught us to obey orders. Then it was time to move out and make room for the next group of soon-to-be soldiers.

All of us were separated from each other. They shipped us in different directions. I ended up at Fort Dix in New Jersey. I was assigned as a Supply Clerk with the 90$^{th}$ General Hospital. The officers in Supply were a great bunch of people to work with, especially the Supply Sergeant. He was Bill Grooms, a little short "Dutchman" from Pennsylvania. We became good friends and took passes together. We dated two sisters in Trenton, New Jersey. He married the one he was dating before we went to England. I escaped.

I was at fort Dix for about six months before leaving for an overseas assignment. We packed up and boarded a train for New York City and the boat docks. There we boarded a French troop carrier called the *Ile-de-France*. We were about two days out to sea when we suddenly turned back toward New York. I was sort of glad because the main course of our meals was always cabbage. I didn't know there was so much cabbage in the world.

I later found out that a fire in the engine room of the ship had made us turn back. I think that ship didn't make any more troop trips. I read after the war that it was used to make a movie where the ship was destroyed. (Good riddance.) We unloaded on Christmas Eve. We were dirty and beardy, and as we marched to the train people were cheering us because they thought we were returning from combat in Africa. They handed us gifts of wine, whiskey, etc.

We went to some camp (I never knew the name) for a couple of days. Then, we were loaded back on a train headed back to New York. This time we were to board the Queen Elisabeth, the English tourist ship, the largest such ship in the world at that time. Over 15,000 troops were on this ship. It sailed alone while most troop ships had escorts to protect them from the German submarines. We went by way of Iceland where the subs couldn't travel because of the ice. The ship sort of zigzagged its course. If there was a sub, it would be hard to set its sights on us. It took us seven days to reach Ireland.

We had air support when we entered open waters in the Irish Sea. Small boats ferried us from the Queen Elisabeth to shore. The ship was too large for docking. We were put on small English trains and taken to a town just across the Scottish border. I believe the name was Chester. We only spent a couple of weeks; there then we boarded the train again and went to Manchester, England. This stop was for a short stay also. We then moved to a small place just outside Worcester called Malvern. This was kind of a tourist retreat. It was near what they called mountains. We would have called them hills back home.

While I was stationed at Malvern Hills, one of my duties was to go along with a laundry detail to Birmingham. I had to check-in and check-out our laundry. We used a large business called Court Steam Laundry to do our laundry. Most of its employees were women, as all the able-bodied men were off in the military service. This meant just one thing—there were lots of pretty young English girls around. Our laundry detail (truck drivers and loaders) started dating some of them.

I met and dated one of these girls, and I have never forgotten her name or where she lived at in Birmingham. Her name was Brenda. The last time I saw her was the week before we were moved to Wales. I had the mess hall cooks prepare me a picnic lunch. Brenda came to the town of Worcester near where I was stationed. I met her at the train station, and we found a nice place on the river bank to have our picnic lunch. The time came too soon for her to catch the train back to Birmingham. We walked to the station where I bid her goodbye not knowing that this would be the last time I would ever see her.

I met many other girls while in Europe (England, France, Germany, Luxemburg, and Belgium). I didn't remember any of their full names or their addresses, but I could never forget this pretty young English girl, Brenda. I always thought that I would be going back through England after the War was over, but we were put on ships and sent straight back to the USA. After I was discharged from the Army, I wrote a few letters to Brenda, but I never did get any answers. I finally gave up on trying to locate her. I always hoped for the best for her, that she would be protected from the many bombings that were taking place. Someday in the future, if I can manage it, I will take a trip to England and try to locate her or some of her family.

We were at Malvern Hills for about two months, and then off we went again, this time to a tourist resort town called Llandundno in Wales. It was on the Irish Sea. This was great—people who came here for vacation were only allowed one week's stay, and most of the ones who visited were women. We could change girlfriends every week and sometimes more often. I met a girl from Liverpool, England. She was really cool (and pretty). She told me a sad story about how she was mistreated, hungry, and lots of other bad things. I believed her.

We were in Wales for only three weeks. Toward the end of our stay, we began to down-size, getting rid of everything we could do without. One thing it turned out we didn't need was our gas masks. They were all to be turned in to Supply. We had two large truck loads of them to turn-in. I was given an address in Liverpool to take them to. I had two men to come along with me to do the unloading. We found the warehouse easily. One truck was unloaded, and I asked the driver to take me to an address. This was the address of the girl I met in Wales who gave me the sad story.

We easily found the house. It was a stately home with a traditional stone wall, a big iron gate, a flower garden, and every thing else. The driver waited in the truck while I went to the front door. I banged the big lion's head door knocker, and a lady came to the door. I explained that I was looking for a girl, and I said Molly Dillon (not her real name). She said that no one by that name lived there. A girl walked from behind the lady and said, "It's okay, Mother. Hi, Charles," she said. It was Molly. She asked me to come in, and we went into what she called a study. She began to explain who she was and why she made up that sad story about her life. She said she was married but that her husband had been gone for two years, and she was lonely. We said goodbye, and I promised to write her.

When we were packed up we boarded a train again and headed to a seaport town called South Hampton. We were given tents in a camp run by the English Army. It was completely fenced in with barbed wire. No one was to go out.

I found the Supply room and became friends with the Supply Sergeant, just killing time. One of the soldiers was all excited. "I'm going on leave. I'm going home. Been gone for two years."

"Where're you from?" I asked.

"Liverpool," he said.

"I know a sweet pretty girl in Liverpool," I said.

"Give me a letter, and I'll get it to her," he said.

Something deep down told me to change the subject. After the soldier left on his way to Liverpool, I asked the Sergeant what the soldier's name was.

"Corporal Dillon" (not his real name, either), he said.

I had to sit down. I had just come close to getting a good whipping by a big English corporal, Molly's husband.

# THE WAR

We were awakened at midnight, loaded into trucks, and taken straight to the docks where ships were waiting for us. We were loaded onto ships until there was standing room only. The English Channel was very rough that morning. The ship was a small one and was rising and falling with every wave. We were finally on our way. It was "D Day" plus five. An announcement came over the ship intercom telling us that we were on our way to France. The Germans had been pushed back, and we would land at Utah Beach.

It was beginning to get light, and you could see the outline of land in the far-off distance. We went in as far as the ship could go, and rope webs were thrown over the side. We had to climb down to the landing craft that were waiting below. They were small: each would carry about fifty soldiers with their equipment. They were bobbing up and down more than the ship. We started down the rope mats not looking up nor turning back. Soldiers were losing their helmets, back-packs, and anything that wasn't fastened down to the body really well. Lots of things that were left behind from the first soldiers who went ashore on the first day were floating around in the water. You could see that getting ashore had been really tough.

The landing craft rammed into the sand quite a ways from land. We had gone in at low tide. The front end of the boat was a big gate. It was let down until the end of the landing craft was wide open, and we hit the water. It was deep enough to be above our waist. There was nothing to do but keep moving toward dry land. We were lucky: The Germans had been pushed back to St. Lo, and we didn't have to dodge bullets. We only had the cold water and the debris floating around everywhere to put up with. The small craft took us in as far as they could and would have to sit grounded until high tide came to lift tem off the sand bottom. Then they could go to deeper water and bring in more loads of men.

What I saw on that day was nothing short of a miracle. How could anyone get on that beach with all the pill boxes on the coast? These were fortified gun emplacements with walls and tops that were at least four feet thick. Nothing could bust them. Wire rolls and other obstacles were also strewn about. The ground was covered with abandoned and damaged equipment, both German and American. At this point there was no time to try to recover it. It could wait.

We finally got together as a group and started inland. We stopped in a field at Carentan about five miles from St. Lowe where General Patton's Third Army was trying to take the town. We were not assigned to any outfit at this time. We each buddied up with someone, and between the two of us we pitched a pup tent. We were given "K rations" for our meals. Some of the meals were okay. You never knew what was in the package until you opened it. The cheese, eggs, potted ham, and beans were all right. I never liked the stew—it was too greasy to eat cold. We also got three or four cigarettes and a chocolate bar. Sometimes this was better than going hungry.

The next morning when I was looking around, I saw a very large field that was turned into a graveyard. It was estimated that there were twenty thousand solders buried there. There were white crosses as far as you could see. Also, there were huge piles of shoes and clothing nearby. I'm sure these belonged to those who were buried there. I found a pair of trooper boots my size, took off my old stiff boots, threw them into the pile, and put on the softer boots. I wore these for the next year or so.

My unassigned status didn't last long. On the third day I was assigned to a twenty-five-man crew who were to drive in the "Red Ball Express." This is what the conveyors that carried supplies from Cherbourg to the front lines was called. Cherbourg was a shipping port where cargo ships could dock. The vehicles we were given to deliver to the front were packed in England. We didn't know what we were hauling. There was only room for one person, a driver, in each vehicle.

I was on this assignment until we reached Metz France. I then was assigned to a Military Police unit. Our duty was to take prisoners back to stockades in France. Lots of times we had to use the German prisoners to build their own stockades. One cold winter day I had about fifteen prisoners holding them for a pick-up crew to come and get them and take them to a stockade farther south. The day went by, and no one came to get the prisoners until nearly dark that evening. I became so cold I was numb, and my feet were frost-bitten. I came down with pneumonia and was put in the hospital at Verdun. I was given penicillin shots every four hours for two days and then sent back to my unit.

I was assigned as a guard to a stockade near a little town named Bar le Duc. This was good duty. We were on duty for twelve hours and off duty twelve hours if nothing came up that required more men. We were living in squad tents with four men per tent. We were near a canal that was used for shipping. The Germans strafed the canal to try to stop barges on the canal. Sometimes they missed and hit our tents, but they never came close to the stockade.

Things were going pretty well until the Germans made their last counter-attack, known as the "Battle of the Bulge." Everyone who could be spared was sent to the Bulge. I missed being on the list of those to go, and I was put on duty at the stockade twenty-four hours a day. The weather was miserable, with snow, fog, and cold, so air support couldn't help. Visibility was so poor that the Air Force planes couldn't see where help was needed.

These conditions lasted for over a week, and then the sun came out. There were clear skies, and the Allied air attack began. The sky was black with airplanes—bombers, fighters, and everything. They flew continuously all day long. The Germans were pushed back, killed, or captured.

The war was near an end in Europe, and it wasn't long afterwards that the Germans gave up and called it quits. We began to let the prisoners go back home. Plans were being made for occupation units to stay in Germany. Because I wasn't married, they sent me to a training class for the occupation. This training lasted about four weeks. Afterwards, I told the commanding officer that I wanted to go home and didn't want to stay in the Army.

Those going back to the United States were given departure schedules. We were given priority points depending on whether we had dependants, how long we had been in service, how long we had been overseas, and some other factors. My priority points put me in about the middle of the list. We were assigned to camps that had the name of cigarettes. I was at Camp Camel. I was about to board ship when orders came to send a company that hadn't been over there very long back to the States. They were to be a part of a victory parade in New York City.

My group was loaded on a train and sent to a port in Belgium. We stayed there another six to eight weeks, and then we boarded a Liberty Ship. These ships carried only 1500 men. They were made mostly of wood. Sailing in them was quite different from sailing in the ship I came over on, the Queen Elisabeth.

It had been over twenty-eight months since I had eaten a hotdog or had any milk. I volunteered for KP duty on the ship so I could have all the milk I wanted. They didn't have any hotdogs, but did have plenty of milk. I don't remember how many pint cartons I drank on my first day at KP—ten or more, I think.

Finally we docked in New York, and from there we were sent to a camp in Virginia. I wasn't there long enough to know its name. While there I lined up to make a telephone call to my former boss in Norfolk to ask about coming back to work with his company. After about an hour of waiting in line, it was my turn to use the phone. I gave the operator the number, and she told me that the line was busy. I wasn't about to wait another hour to try again. It seemed that everyone was calling home or somewhere.

From the camp in Virginia I was sent to Fort Bragg, North Carolina, the same place I had started from several years ago. There I was to be processed for separation from the Army. Although I protested, I had to stay for an extra day because they had found a spot on my lungs. It was probably a scar from the pneumonia I had in France. An older officer who was processing me said that I was being assigned a disability claim number. It was to be a "zero" claim. He informed me that someday when I was older I might need to open the claim. I have never filed a claim, but the claim number would get me any medical treatment that I might need in the future.

Finally, I was a civilian again and was on my way home.

# GETTING MARRIED

I was twenty years old when I went into the Service and twenty-four (1942-1946) when I was discharged. I was going home to re-enlist, but not in the Army. I was going to get married.

After I finally got my discharge, they gave me a ride to the bus station where I bought a ticket to Lexington, North Carolina. This was where my mom and dad were living at the time. Dad had quit working at the paper mill in Canton, and he was now working in a cotton mill. Why he left a good-paying job in the paper mill to work in a cotton mill, I don't know.

I spent only one night with my family, and the next morning I headed to the bus station and got a ticket to Canton. This was where the girl I was going to marry lived. After arriving in Canton, I went to my brother's house. He lived in the Thickety Community. It was after midnight when I reached his house.

My brother, TJ, was at work. He was working the third shift (11 P.M. to 7 A.M.) in the paper mill. I knocked on his door, and his wife, Alveta, came to the door. She wanted to know who was knocking on the door at this hour. I told her, and she opened the door and let me in. I had known Alveta since grade school.

TJ rode a bus to work, so his car was at home. Alveta told me to take the car and meet TJ when he finished work. Also, she told me that Marie Young, my future bride, was working at Enka, a rayon mill near Asheville, and that she would be at Crossroad Hill to catch a bus to work at about six that morning. Marie had to walk from her house in Buckeye Cove to catch her work bus because it didn't go by where she lived. I took the car and was at Crossroad Hill at five-thirty.

Marie didn't know I was out of the Army. No one living out in the country had a telephone at that time. Only the city people had them, so news traveled pretty slowly. It was to be a surprise for her. She came up to Crossroad Hill at about five forty-five, and it was still pretty dark. I stepped from behind the car and said, "Hi." This scared Marie pretty much. I said, "This is Charles." Then she recognized my voice, and her fear was gone.

After we got re-acquainted, I asked Marie to send word to her boss by someone on the bus that she wouldn't be coming in to work that day. She arranged this, and we got into the car to go pick up TJ, who would be getting off from work at seven. We parked near where the work buses picked up their passengers. When TJ came out, he, too, was surprised to see me.

We went to his house where Alveta had cooked us a big country breakfast. We didn't eat a whole lot because we were still a little bit excited about seeing each other again. After eating, TJ and I went to bed to get some sleep. He had worked all night, and I hadn't slept for about twenty-four hours.

Around noon TJ and I got out of bed. Marie was still there, and she and Alveta had everything worked out. All the plans were made: we would wait a week before getting married. This would give Marie time to quit her job at Enka and make preparations for our wedding. Also, this would allow TJ to arrange to take a few days of vacation.

Since I was still wearing my Army uniform, I needed some new clothes for the wedding. I needed a suit. I had never owned one in my entire life. TJ took me to Asheville where we found a men's clothing store. I picked out a double-breasted blue serge suit that was pretty fancy, I thought. It even had a vest that went with the coat and pants. The price wasn't too bad either, about fifteen dollars. I also bought a white shirt to go with the suit. TJ was going to give me a necktie. The fifteen dollars seemed like a lot to me, but what the heck? This was for the biggest day of my life. Why not splurge a little?

We decided not to have a church wedding but something simple instead. We would go to Georgia and get married. The reason for this was that North Carolina had a two-week waiting period from the time you bought a marriage license until you were married. In Georgia you bought the license and were married all on the same day in the same building by a tobacco-chewing justice of the peace. It was nothing fancy, all business. I would guess that the whole thing took a full fifteen minutes altogether.

On Saturday morning I took TJ's car and went to the Young's house in Buckeye Cove. Marie was all packed and ready for the trip to Georgia. We went back to get Alveta and TJ. He was going to drive on the trip. We went to Clayton, Georgia, as planned, and everything took place as expected, tobacco-chewing JP and all.

For our honeymoon we went to Atlanta. It was after dark when we arrived. We didn't have any reservations, so we started looking for a hotel. We found one that had two vacancies. Hotels at that time didn't have a bathroom in each room. There was a shared bathroom on each floor. Anyhow, this was more than we were used to back home. There the "bathroom" was an over-sized washtub and a little building out in the field.

The next morning bright and early there was a knock on our door. It was TJ. He told us that he and Alveta were leaving to go back home to Canton. We were on our own, all alone, a long ways from home without any plans for what we would do next. We didn't worry. We were happy and enjoying the big city. But there was one problem: we were getting short on funds.

We started thinking about what we would do next. We decided to take a bus to Charlotte, North Carolina. This wasn't too far from Lexington where my family lived. We decided that there was enough money left for us to spend a night at a hotel in Charlotte. The hotel where we stayed was quite new, and there was a complete bath in our room. We were living "uptown."

We only spent one night at the fancy hotel and then headed to my parents' house in Lexington. We had a short visit there, and then we took the Trailways bus to Canton. We spent several nights at Marie's parents' house near Canton.

I had made up my mind several years ago to go back to school. It dawned on me while I was in the Army that to get ahead you had to be prepared. I saw this first-hand in the Army. All the city boys who had better educations than some of us so-called hillbillies got all the promotions and good jobs. We got the ones that were left. These were usually the hard and dirty jobs.

Since I had applied for a trade school in Chicago, we didn't want to tie ourselves down until we knew where I would be working. My great aunt lived alone and wanted us to live with her until I left for school. This worked out perfectly for everyone. Aunt Grace gave us a place to live, and I did several jobs for her that needed done around the house that she couldn't do herself. Aunt Grace's third husband had been dead for several years. I believe he was quite a bit older than she was. She drew his Spanish-American War pension, and that was her sole source of income. It was not much, but it was enough to buy the few things she needed to survive.

I was accepted as a student at Coyne Electrical School in Chicago, and the time for my enrollment drew near. I was going ahead to Chicago by myself to find and rent an apartment that would be large enough for Marie, Alveta, TJ, and me because TJ was also going to attend the school, too. We were all going to live together to save on expenses. I took the bus to Chicago alone. I didn't want to leave Marie, but this was a part of our plan. I was going to get a place to live, and she would come when TJ and Alveta came. It would only be three weeks.

I was pretty busy in school, and the three weeks went by really fast. The school work was pretty hard for me. Our instructors told us that they would tell us something one time and only once, and that we would get out of the school exactly what we put into it.

We were attending school under the GI Bill. The government paid all our school expenses and some of our living expenses. It didn't take long to use up the few dollars I had saved, and I didn't receive any of the support pay for three months. This meant that Marie and Alveta had to get jobs. They went to work pretty close to our apartment in a factory that made watch and clock crystals. They worked in the shipping department. Although there wasn't as much traffic then (1946) as nowadays, Marie and Alveta were afraid to cross the wide, four-lane streets. TJ or I would take them across the streets before we went to school.

I finished school three weeks ahead of TJ, so Marie and I headed back to Canton. We weren't sure where we would settle down, because the school placed its graduates in jobs in many places. We decided we would take our time about making a decision. In the meantime, I filled out an application for a job in the Electrical Department of the Champion Paper Mill in Canton. TJ did the same when he came back home. A friend of ours had built a four-room box house on his farm for one of his hired hands. I asked him to rent it to Marie and me for a few months. It wasn't much, but it was affordable at twelve dollars a month.

We were living there when one day Mance Tate, a security guard from the paper mill, came to our house and left word with Marie that I was to come to the mill the next day for a job in their Electrical Department. As I have mentioned before, there were no telephones out in the country then, so the paper mill had one of their security officers take messages to anyone who they wanted to contact. I accepted the job and went to work immediately.

I was helping one of the older electricians install lighting fixtures in the YMCA building that the mill had built for the town when Lee McElrath, the personnel manager, appeared. He called aside the fellow I was working with, Gerald Mashburn, and asked him who I was. Gerald told him that I was Charles Fletcher.

The personnel manager left us, went back to his office, and called in the guard Mance Tate. He told him that he had asked him to get that Fletcher boy who went to Coyne Electrical School and put him to work. Mance told him that this is a Fletcher boy, and he did go to Coyne Electrical School.

"Well," Lee said. "We can't fire this boy because Gerald said he was a good worker. Go get the other Fletcher boy and put him to work, too."

I was known by the name of "Mistake" for quite awhile after that. They later called me "Big Bones" and TJ "Little Bones." We were both pretty skinny in those days.

Here I am at this point in my life with a good wife, a good job, and a house to live in all in less than a year. What more could I ask for? I'd call this "moving on."

# RAISING A FAMILY

When Marie and I had been married for over a year, we talked about starting a family. Everyone needs some children around to keep things from being so calm around the house. So, soon the first one was on the way. Things went really smooth. Marie didn't have any problems. I was busy working. I worked a lot of overtime. We were planning on building a new house pretty soon for our new family.

There was a tract of land that lots of people had tried to buy, but the owner wouldn't sell. It was a beautiful, four-acre tract that belonged to some good friends of mine. I grew up with their two boys and had spent a lot of time at their home. This piece of land was sort of an odd part of their farm. It was off by itself separate from the rest of the farm land.

I paid Mr. and Mrs. Brown (Oscar and Sally) a visit one evening and asked them about buying this piece of land. Oscar spoke first and said, "I don't think we ought to sell this land. Our boys may want to build a house there some day."

As was the case in a lot of the families in the mountains of Western North Carolina, the woman of the house was larger than the man and usually had the last word in decisions. This was one of those cases, and was I so glad it was.

Sally spoke up. "Well, Oscar," she said. "We have lots of other land that our boys could build on, and besides this little piece of land don't fit in with our other land. It sets out by itself. I think we should let Charles have it. He would make a fine neighbor."

"All right," Oscar said.

"How much money do you want for it?" I asked.

"How much can you afford?" Sally said.

"Well," I said. "I have fifteen hundred that I saved while I was in the Army."

"That would be enough," Sally said. "We'll get the deed made out to you and Marie."

I felt like hugging Sally's neck but decided not to overdo it. I just said, "Thank you, Sally. I'll be your best neighbor."

Marie and I decided to wait until the baby was born before starting to build our house. This would be another four or five months. There was no rush because I didn't have any money left after paying the Browns for the land anyhow.

One night when I was working shift work in the paper mill and was on the third shift (11 P.M. to 7 A.M.), one of our neighbors came to the mill and said that Marie's baby was about to be born and that I needed to come home. He took me home, and I borrowed a car from my brother-in-law and took Marie to the hospital in Waynesville. The hospital called our doctor, and he came to the hospital. I asked how long it would be, and he said that we would just have to let nature take its course. Nature took its time, too. It was the next afternoon before Marie had the baby. It was a big baby boy. I was really proud. Every father dreams of having a boy who he can share his life with. I got my wish. Marie had to stay in the hospital for a few days after giving birth. That was the custom back then.

We were still living in the little twelve-dollar box house when Gary was born. (This was our first baby's name.) It's hard to understand how we managed to keep warm in this house. It had been built with green lumber, and once the lumber dried it shrank to a smaller size. We could see grass growing under the house through cracks in the floor. I guess we were tough like all the others in the mountains of Western North Carolina in those days.

It was time to start building the new house, but we still didn't have the money for it. I had talked to the power house superintendent at the mill. He was chairman of the local savings and loan association. He said that to get a loan I would have to meet with the board of directors to get approval and that I needed some sort of a plan.

I met with the board at their next meeting, and I explained how I wanted to borrow money to build our house. I told them the land that I owned was paid for and that the value of it was well over fifteen hundred dollars. I told them I would give them a deed of trust on the property if they would loan me one thousand dollars to use for buying materials and paying carpenters to start building a house. Then, when this money was gone, they could deposit another thousand in my bank account to be used toward building. Thus, the value of their security would always be greater than their investment. This plan of operation would continue until the job is completed, and they would have a lien on the house and land as security for their loan.

The manager of the savings and loan company said that this would be a construction loan, and they had never made such a loan before. He didn't think they should loan me the money.

Bill Mitchell, the chairman of the board, spoke up in his South Georgia drawl, saying, "I don't see anything wrong with this here boy's plan. Just because we haven't done a loan of this kind before is no reason that we can't loan him the money."

The board all agreed with Bill, and I got up and thanked everyone. Roy Patten, the manager, followed me out and asked when I wanted the first thousand. I asked him to deposit in my checking account at the bank as soon as possible. I told him that I would let him know when this was gone, and he could make another deposit.

We now had money to get started. First, we had to find carpenters to build the house. It so happened that one of my great uncles was a pretty good carpenter, and he agreed to build the house. He would need help, so he got my mother's brother to help him for one dollar an hour.

I took my house plans to a local lumber yard, and they made a list of the lumber I would need. I didn't buy from them but instead went to a man named Thea Allen for my lumber. He could furnish all the lumber for fifteen dollars per thousand board feet. This was a good price, so the deal was made with him.

I needed a bulldozer to dig a basement, and I hired one for five dollars an hour. We were to have a full basement. Next I hired a block mason to lay the walls.

The well for water was one of my projects. I had experience at well digging from digging the Wines' well several years before. I would dig a few feet every day in the evenings and on the days I didn't work at the mill. I had to hire a Trentham boy to haul dirt up after digging down about six feet. I hit solid rock and a real good stream of water at thirty feet deep. I had to put a three-foot tile in so the water would stay clear. The water was crystal clear.

I also did the electrical work, finishing the hardwood floors, and the painting myself. We would do the yard later after moving in.

When we were ready to move in, the move wasn't a big job because we didn't have much furniture or belongings. We had bed, a cooking stove, a wood-burning heater, and a table with four chairs. We didn't need the heater because I had installed an oil furnace in the new house.

With all the things that were going on in our lives, it would be four years before our next child was born. I built a barn and bought some cows to raise veal calves. I was doing electrical work for other people and going to night school a couple of nights a week. Marie was very busy also churning milk, canning a couple of hundred cans of fruits and vegetables, and feeding the hogs we raised to supply our winter meat. She also had a couple of milk customers. So, our family growth was kind of slow.

Taking a vacation was nearly out of the question. I had bought an old Plymouth panel truck to get back and forth to the mill and to haul my electrical materials. A friend who worked with me was from the coast of North Carolina, and his dad was a commercial fisherman. The friend's father had an ocean-going boat, and he said that his dad would let me go deep-sea fishing on his boat if I would come to Homestead where his fishing boat was docked. So, we decided to take a vacation trip to the seacoast in my old panel truck.

Gary, our first-born son, was still a baby, but we set out to travel to the ocean. Marie packed us some food to eat on the way. We invited one of my nieces to go along, and off we all went in that old panel truck that had lots of things wired on it to keep them from falling off. We didn't worry. We were young and happy; that was all that counted.

The motels then were a one-room affair with the sink and toilet along the wall and no curtains to hide behind when using the toilet.— You just had to ask your roommates to turn their heads. I went fishing, and then we went back to Canton. Marie and Betty had enjoyed the trip. Most people didn't travel very far from their homes at that time, so this was an unusual treat for us.

Some work on the new house was still going on when I got the news that our second child was well on its way. This was good news. We wanted more children. Everything to do with the birth of our second son went about the same as with the first except that Marie was in labor so long that the doctors advised her not to have any more children. We named our new boy "Dean." (To be exact it was "Charles Dean," but we decided to use only the "Dean" part.)

Now I had two small boys at my heels when I was home. They had to help with everything that I did. For example, Gary once helped me de-horn a young cow I had just bought. We did this after I came home from work one evening. We went to the barn. I tied the cow's head up close to the wall, put the de-horn clipper over the cow's horn, and clipped it off. Blood was spraying all over the place until I applied tar to stop the bleeding. Gary left the barn crying and screaming, running to his mother for comfort. He wouldn't go near the barn for quite some time after that. The sight of blood still upsets him.

We were blessed. We had two fine young boys, owned our own home, and even had splurged and bought the first television in the community. I also bought a new 1951 Chevrolet with an automatic transmission. All this was ours. We didn't owe anyone anything. God had blessed us. Marie and I had worked hard to make all this possible.

# MOVING TO TENNESSEE

We had a new 1951 Chevy, and work had slowed down around the house, so we started thinking about taking a vacation. We thought of writing a letter to Harley Panhorst and his wife, Mamie, who lived in St. Louis to see if it would be all right to visit them. Harley was an Army buddy of mine during WWII. We had been keeping in touch by letter ever since we left the Army. The Panhorsts had invited us for a visit several times.

We got word back from them really quickly and started planning a trip to Missouri. Our niece, Carolyn, Marie's oldest sister's daughter, wanted to go along with us. This was good because she was twelve years old, and she would be a great help to us. She could help take care of our youngest son, Dean, who was nearly one-year-old.

Everything was set for the trip. We would leave on a Friday afternoon after I got off from work at four o'clock. We planned to travel as far as Cleveland, Tennessee, and spend the night. Little did we know that this trip was to lead up to our moving to Tennessee later on.

Everything was packed in the car when I arrived home at four-thirty. All I had to do was get on the road. We drove until just before dark and stopped at a picnic table at the Parksville Lake dam. We had a fast picnic and continued traveling to Cleveland. It was dark when we arrived, and we started looking for a motel to stay in. We couldn't find a motel in Cleveland. There was a hotel in Cleveland, but we didn't know that it was there.

We kept driving north on US Highway 11 until we were in Athens, Tennessee. There we asked around about a motel and were given directions to the only one nearby. It was a six-unit motel. Each unit was a separate one-room building. Each unit had a bed, a wash basin, and a commode set out in plain view over in a corner. It didn't have any privacy at all. We all spent our first night on the road in one of these units.

It rained all that night, but the rain stopped before we left the next morning. We had to go back toward Cleveland to continue our trip. When we came to Calhoun, Tennessee, a small village on the banks of the Hiwassee River, we saw a paper mill under construction. An Englishman named Sir Eric Bowater was having the mill built.

The site had an office where the first seven of the paper mill's employees worked, and I stopped there and asked to talk to the person who would be in charge of the paper mill electrical department. A secretary took me to an office and introduced me to Mr. John Osborne who had been hired to be superintendent of the electrical department. I asked him about the possibility of employment. He asked me many questions about my background in the electrical field. He told me that the mill didn't yet have job application forms, but he would mail me one as soon as they were available. He said that they would need people like me, someone with experience working in a paper mill.

After that we got back on the road again. It was a very warm day, and we kept all the windows on the car open in order to keep cool. Cars back then didn't come with air conditioners installed in them. Women then didn't care if their hair was blown about by the wind. Comfort was more important than looks.

We made good time on the road but didn't get to St. Louis that day. We found another of the one-room motels and spent the night there. We had a short trip on in to St. Louis the next day. We arrived before noon in east St. Louis. It was on the east bank of the Mississippi River. The Panhorst family lived on the west side of the river. We found a pretty good motel that had a separate room for the bathroom, complete with a bathtub, and settled in.

I called the Panhorst home from the motel. Mrs. Panhorst answered the telephone. I told her where we were, and she insisted that we get a refund from the motel and come stay at their house. I asked for directions, and she said that Harley would come to the motel and guide us to their house. It wasn't long before he came to where we were, and we followed him to their house.

We had a very good week with them. Harley was working part of each day. He was superintendent of the St. Louis parks administration. We visited the zoo, the baseball stadium, and lots of other places that week. We invited the Panhorsts to come visit us the next summer.

We had a pleasant, enjoyable trip back home. We were glad to be back in North Carolina and to be able to rest up from our trip. We were pretty tired when we got back. The Panhorsts did visit us the next summer. We took them on many trips through the mountains.

One night at about seven o'clock I received a phone call from Calhoun, Tennessee. (I had a telephone installed in the new house by this time.) It was from Mr. Osborne. He told me he was sending an employment application form. He also wanted me to come to Calhoun for an interview. I explained that the only time I could come would be on a Saturday. That was all right with him, and we set a date for the interview.

When I made the interview visit, we toured the paper mill to be, which still wasn't completed. I returned home to Canton and didn't think much about the possibility of going to Tennessee to work. A few weeks later I received another call from Mr. Osborne who told me he wanted me to come back to talk some more.

I went for the second interview. This time my brother, TJ, went with me. I spent most of the day looking around the mill and talking with Mr. Osborn. He told me that he had to make a decision about choosing an electrical foreman from among about twenty people wanting the job. I was one of three people he was considering for the job. He told me that he would get in touch with me about his hiring decision shortly.

I soon heard back from him. He had decided on a Mr. Buchheit for the job. He had chosen him because he was older, and he had more paper machine experience than I did. I thanked him for my interview visits. This wasn't all, though. He wanted me to take a job as an electrician. He said that the pay was about the same as I was getting now, but that there would be a great future for me at Bowater Paper Corporation. Chances for a better future would be greater in a new mill.

I asked when he would want me to come to work, and he said that he'd like me to come to work as soon as I could. I told him that I wouldn't leave the paper mill at Canton without giving a two-week notice. He agreed to that. The next day I turned in my notice at Champion Paper Corporation.

After that I received another call from Bowater. This time it was from their personnel department. They said that they required me to get a physical examination from a doctor before employment and that they had overlooked telling me about this. I was to send them the names and telephone numbers of three doctors, and they would tell me which one to go to. I gave them this information, and they picked a physician for me to go see for the exam.

The two weeks went by, and I left for my new job in Tennessee. Marie was going to stay in Canton until the school year was over, and then she and the children would move. Gary was attending Beaverdam Elementary School, the same one that I had attended.

I stayed with a friend in Athens, Tennessee, until I could build or rent a house. I would go back to Canton every Friday and return to my job on Monday mornings. Construction at the mill in Calhoun wasn't finished, and I didn't have anything much to do but to look around the place at that time.

We decided to build a house instead of rent a place. With the help of one of the Bowater officials, I located and bought four acres of land on US Highway 11. The land was located halfway between Cleveland and Calhoun. We had house plans already, and I hired a builder, Mr. Best, from Athens, to build a new house.

When everything was ready, Bowater made arrangements for a moving company to move our belonging from North Carolina to Tennessee. I brought Marie, Gary, and Dean, and we now lived in Tennessee.

# THE PAPER MILL

We were in Tennessee, the paper mill was completed, and my new job had begun.

The paper mill hired twenty electricians. We were paired into two-man teams. Our job was to check out all the electrical equipment to make sure it worked properly before we started up the entire mill and began making paper. This was quite a job for twenty people, especially since about half of them were former construction electricians and did not know anything about an electric circuit. They just stood around looking at each other. The ones who actually knew how to check out and start up electrical equipment were working fifteen or more hours a day, seven days a week.

I was never home. I would leave for a few hours to take Marie to buy groceries. She had never learned to drive a car. I would call a grocery store where I was acquainted with the owner and have him keep his store open so we could shop. The store owner's name was Toby Taylor. He was a good businessman and later had one of the first supermarkets in Cleveland.

Gary had started to school at Charleston Elementary School. Marie needed to learn how to drive the car in order to take care of the family. I didn't have much time away from the mill. I started taking off from work on Sundays, and this gave me a chance to teach her how to drive.

We had found a church that we wanted to join. It was North Cleveland Baptist Church located on US Highway 11 in Cleveland. We began the driving lessons after church and lunch on Sundays. First, Marie practiced in the large parking lot at Bowater. Then we went driving on the back roads where there wasn't much traffic.

She soon had driving under control, and the next thing was for her to get her driver's license. She had studied the Tennessee driver's manual for her written test, but she would also have to take a road test. The road test was given by a Tennessee Highway Patrol officer. I picked a day when I could be off work, and we went to the testing site. She passed the written test and drove an officer around town for the road test in our car. The place that I had parked was between two cars. I knew she couldn't get the car back in this tight space, so I had the person who was parked on the end of the block to move his car into the tight space. This allowed Marie to park in the end space, and that would be easy. I stood at the curb and kept anyone from taking this space. This worked out well—she had no trouble parking, and she got her license.

At the mill, we finally finished getting things running and started the paper machines rolling. At this time the paper machines were running at speeds of over twenty-five hundred feet a minute. This was a record speed. There was a great demand for newsprint, and the two machines couldn't meet the demand. The company immediately started making plans to expand.

I was finally getting some time away from the mill, so we began to explore this new country we had moved to. One of our first trips was to Harriman, Tennessee, to locate an army buddy of mine. He was a part American Indian whose name was Clarence Brazille. We located him with the help of a telephone directory. We had a short visit with him and returned to Cleveland.

The temperature on the day of our trip was about one hundred degrees, and our car didn't have air conditioning. Marie began one of her many periods of wishing she were back in the cool mountains of North Carolina. The hot weather didn't bother the boys or me, but she often complained about the climate in Tennessee.

Everything was about what you would expect with a growing family. We experienced the usual things like the children getting sick or injured. Dean, my younger son, was the bad luck child as far as getting injured. I guess this was because he was so active.

One Sunday we had been to Harrison Bay State Park for a picnic and to let the boys swim. After we came home, Gary was chasing Dean around the house, and then everything suddenly became quiet. In a few minutes here came Dean holding his arm.

"Dad," he said, "I think I hurt my arm."

While he was running, he had hit his arm against our picnic table. It looked pretty bad to me, so I took him to the emergency room at the hospital in Cleveland. We found out that his arm was broken just above the wrist and that the bone would have to be re-set and that he would have to have a plaster cast put on his arm.

While a nurse held his shoulders, the emergency room doctor gave his arm a quick yank and a twist, and the broken bone was back in place. I'm sure that it hurt Dean, but he only hollered, "Ouch!" one time. Then they put a cast on his arm from his elbow all the way to his wrist. He had to keep the cast on his arm for six weeks. This didn't stop him from doing the things he wanted to do, though.

Later on, while he was in high school, Dean broke his ankle while playing basketball. This also required a cast from his knee down to his toes. Gary also had a few bruises and scratches but never had any serious injuries like Dean. He was lucky as far as being injured goes.

The mill's new No. Three paper machine was well on its way to being completed. I had the job of coordinator and inspector on this project. I had to make sure that the electrical contractor was doing the work according to Bowater's specifications. This was a very educational assignment for me. I learned more on this job than I could ever learn from studying books. Doing this provided a great advantage for me in later years when I was promoted to the Engineering Department.

Through extension and correspondence schools I completed an industrial electrical engineering course of study. I now had a diploma for what I had been studying for the past fifteen years. When I joined the Engineering Department, there was no opening for an engineer, so I was classified an Electrical Designer. When I entered the

Engineering Department, I explained that I couldn't draw (draft) very well. The chief engineer told me that I wasn't hired to make pretty drawings but that I was needed to design electrical jobs so that they would work properly. He said that if he wanted pretty drawings, he would get someone else to make them. I was relieved. My lettering was readable enough, but not pretty.

It was good that Marie had learned to drive the car. If she hadn't been able to drive, we would have had a big problem. The school in Charleston where Gary and Dean went to school caught fire one night and burned completely down. Our children would have to go to school in Cleveland while a new school was being built at Charleston. This meant that Marie had to drive the boys to school in Cleveland in the mornings and drive there to bring them home everyday after school. The round trip to Cleveland and back was ten miles, and she drove the ten mile trip there and back twice a day.

Since the children were commuting to and from Cleveland five days a week, we decided to sell our house and build a new one in Cleveland. The first family who looked at our house once it was up for sale bought it. They wanted to move in right away, so we found a nice house to rent in Cleveland to live in until we could build our new house.

We found a good lot for sale on Harris Circle. At that time the place was on the edge of town, and living there would sort of be like being in the country. Our new house would be the first one on the street. Water and electrical lines hadn't yet been installed on this street, and it was still a dirt road.

We bought the lot and found a very good building contractor, Mr. Mittal. He took care of everything except the electrical work, and I did the electrical work. The house was soon finished, and we moved in. This was our fourth residence since Marie and I were married. We hoped that this would be our final move.

As expected, Bowater started installation of a fourth paper machine. I was again assigned to be the electrical coordinator on the construction project. This job wasn't too bad. I didn't have to work long hours, so I was home with the family at night and on weekends.

We had lots of company after moving to Tennessee. Relatives and acquaintances from Canton who had never come to visit us when we lived there came to visit us now. We always tried to make them feel welcome. We also made many trips back to Canton to visit Marie's family. It was about a six-hour trip by car from our home in Tennessee to Canton. The roads were crooked and narrow fifty years ago, but we didn't mind them. We were young and happy.

Bowater soon began the start-up of its No. Four paper machine. During start-up I had to work long hours. Everything had to be just right for the machine to make paper. After we began to make paper, I could take time off. Bill Lindsay, owner of Duncan Electric Company, the electrical contractor for this project, had been working long hours during start-up, also. Once everything was running smoothly, he asked me to go fishing with him down in Florida. The fishing trip would be a much-deserved vacation for us. We got permission from the chief engineer to be gone for a week in order to go fishing.

I had never been to Florida, so I was excited about going there. Also, I loved to fish. Bill had all the fishing gear we needed loaded in his car, and he came to my house to pick me up. On the way, we stopped and spent the night in a motel just south of Atlanta. When we entered Florida the next day, we began to see many orange groves. I asked Bill to stop so that I could pick a real orange from a real orange tree.

We were soon at the fish camp where Bill had made reservations for us for a week. The camp was called Beacon 58 Fishing Camp. It was located near where the Kennedy Space Center is today. The Space Center was just being built when we were there. As soon as we were unloaded and had a bite to eat, Bill was ready to start fishing.

The guides had a boat ready for us. It was a small, two-man row boat with a five-horsepower motor. Bill had fished here several times before, so we didn't need a guide. I was afraid. The small boat was tossing about on the waves. We were wearing life jackets, but this didn't calm me down. We stopped and dropped anchor, and Bill began fishing. I wasn't fishing because I was still hanging onto the sides of the boat.

Bill said, "We came all this way to catch some fish, and all you do is hang onto the sides of the boat. Get to fishing."

I finally baited a hook, and threw my line into the water. We were using live shrimp for bait. Wham! I caught something almost immediately. After getting the fish on the boat, we saw that I had caught a sea trout, and it was a beauty. It weighed about six pounds. After that, my fear of ocean waves was gone.

We made two trips out fishing everyday—one in the morning and one after lunch. We caught plenty of fish every time we went out. The guides filleted them and put them in a freezer. When we left to come home, we had over seventy-five pounds of sea trout. I kept some for myself, and Bill took the rest. He had the cook at the Bowater cafeteria fry the fish and make hush-puppies and cole slaw. We then invited all the Electrical Department people at Bowater for the fish fry.

Bowater now had four paper machines running at top speeds, and everyone was back to working regular hours. We all could relax, take some time off, and do some of the things we had looked forward to doing.

# CLEVELAND

Now that I didn't have to be close to the telephone when not at the mill, Marie and the boys could plan things that we could do together—things that we hadn't had time to do since moving to Cleveland. We were beginning to like Cleveland more than we did at first. We had made lots of friends and were visiting and going on picnics and trips with them. We were also joining in more things at church and at the schools where Gary and Dean were attending. We didn't feel so alone anymore.

There is one thing for sure—you don't have a whole lot of idle time on your hands when you are raising a family, especially in our case. We had two young boys. There was a four-year difference in their ages. This caused several problems. For example, Dean couldn't wear hand-me-down clothes that Gary had outgrown. Gary was the more serious one; Dean was full of energy and fun and always up front. I suppose Dean gets his outlook on life from me.

Gary was now in junior high school. Dean was well along in grammar school. There was a difference in their sports, and their homework assignments were miles apart. We helped as much as we could. They didn't ask for too much help.

Dean got the opportunity to attend a private school. This was great for him. The school was founded by the most prominent people in Cleveland, Athens, and the surrounding area. There was a tuition cost, but the school was mostly supported by these people who had extra money and wanted their children to get the best education possible. The public schools, both in the county and in the city, are better today than they used to be. I think the local governments have more money to spend on education today than they had fifty some years ago. This is great. We all benefit from having our future citizens better educated. We all are rewarded by this.

As mentioned before, Dean was the one with all the energy around home and everywhere else. At school he was one of the better basketball players. He was on the first soccer team in Bradley County. (This was at the private Cleveland Day School that he attended.) His teams had to go on long trips to play in competition Atlanta, Knoxville, and other places that required traveling quite a ways.

Gary also was active in things at school. He played on his junior high school's first football team. That team was to become the Cleveland High School team years later, the Cleveland "Blue Raiders." He also started playing football at Bradley County High School. He was on the team that Steve Sloan had left the year before he began. He played in the defensive line because he wasn't afraid to tackle and hit. This cost him later. He made a tackle one day and somehow broke some teeth off. He spent most of the summer getting his teeth fixed. When football practice started in the fall, he didn't go out for the team again. The coach tried to get him to change his mind, but he wouldn't. Shorty Jordan, the coach, came to our house one evening and asked me to talk Gary into rejoining the team. I told him I was not going to pressure him. If he wanted to play, it would be okay. If not, this was okay also. This ended Gary's football playing.

But, guess what? Gary began playing again—no, not football. Of all things, he began playing the bass guitar. He and some of his friends started first, a folk group and, then, a rock-and-roll band. In the end, the band included our preacher's son, Randy, the Guffey's son, Dennis, a saxophone player, a drummer, a singer, and Gary. At first, all the tunes they played sounded the same. Then, their playing got better, and they played for various events and at some high-school dances. They were paid enough to keep up their instruments and buy enough gasoline to get to where they were going to play. Soon, the members of the band went different ways, the band broke up, and this ended Gary's music playing.

While the boys were still attending local schools, one night in September I received an unexpected telephone call at about nine o'clock. It was from my big boss, Mr. Osborne, the man who had talked me into coming to Tennessee. He was now vice president for engineering.

He began by saying, "Charley, can you go to New Zealand for about three to six months? Bowater has built a new paper mill in New Zealand; they're getting ready to start up, and they have asked if you could come down and give them a hand."

"Can I take my family with me?" I asked.

"No. You will have to go alone," he replied.

"I can't give you an answer right now," I said. "I'll let you know next week when you get back from your vacation."

He said, "I need an answer tonight. Mr. Sutton wants an answer tonight. You talk it over with Marie, and call me back. I'm at home."

Marie and I talked it over, and Marie said that she could get along all right with the boys for that long. She told me to call him back and tell him I would go. I really didn't want to leave Marie to take care of the boys alone because the boys were at that difficult stage all boys go though, part adult and part child.

I called Mr. Osborne back, and he said for me to report to Mr. Victor Sutton the next morning, and he would give me the details. Mr. Sutton was an Englishman who came from England with the original team who managed the building of the mill. He was the president and CEO of all of Bowater's operations in North America. The new paper mill in New Zealand was also his responsibility.

When I reported to him, he began by saying that they needed my help very much in New Zealand. He also said that there was some resentment towards Americans down there.

"You go and offer them your help with their problems," he told me. If they accept you, that will be fine. If they try to give you trouble, catch the next airplane leaving New Zealand and come back home. You will have a round-trip ticket. Don't argue or take sides in any dispute."

"Mr. Sutton," I said, "You have about twenty good electrical engineers in the Research and Development Department. One of them could go."

"Damn it," he said. "If I'd wanted one of them to go, I wouldn't have had Johnny call you."

"Well," I said. "I don't own any luggage to take enough clothes to last three months."

"Go and buy whatever you need and charge it to Bowater," he replied.

I thought to myself. *There's no way of getting out of this.*

Mr. Sutton continued, "You will be half-way around the world. You will be on your own. You can't call General Electric or Westinghouse to come give you a hand."

I said, "I can only promise to do the best I can."

"That's all I expect of you. Everything will be all right," he assured me. "Don't mention anything about this to your fellow employees. I will tell them when they need to know," he added.

It just so happened that one of Bowater's engineers from Research and Development was in New Zealand when they received word that I would be coming down under to give them a hand. He came back to Bowater the next week and began to tell others that I would be going. So, the announcement was made.

The secretaries in the Engineering Department began making plans for a surprise going-away party for me. Mary Hybarger, the senior secretary (and my favorite), headed up the planning. She did it up first class. There was a big cake with an airplane and lots of writing on it. Learning that the people I worked with (some of whom I had had disagreements with) thought this well of me humbled me. I was speechless.

The night before I was scheduled to leave, I received a phone call telling me that I was to leave that night and spend the night in Atlanta. The reason for the change in plans was that the weather forecast was for heavy fog the next morning, and Mr. Sutton didn't want me to miss my flight from Atlanta to Los Angeles. He was sending a driver to take me to the Chattanooga Airport to catch the last flight to Atlanta. Reservations were already made at a hotel near the Atlanta Airport. I had the new luggage that I had bought and charged to Bowater all packed and ready, so I was able to leave on short notice.

I had bought the best three-piece set of luggage that I could find. I was told that I would be going first class and I was to act first class. I was told that, after all, I was a representative of Bowater, and the way I conducted myself was a reflection of our company.

The driver was on time. I said a quick goodbye to the family, and I was on my way. I would be telling a lie if I said I wasn't choked up inside and a little bit afraid. I had been far away from home before, but then I didn't leave a wife and two growing young men behind. And, I was going into an unknown situation.

In Atlanta the next morning, I boarded the airplane; we taxied out to the runway to take off, the engines were revved up to high speed, and then all at once they slowed down. The plane turned and went back to the terminal, and the pilot shut the engines down. The captain told us over the intercom that we would have a slight delay and that it was nothing serious.

A crew of four men with a high-lift platform and some sort of equipment came up to the plane. I had a window seat just in front of the wing. I could see what they were doing. They began unbolting, prying, hammering, and I don't know what all. This didn't look too good to me, considering we were about to leave on a three thousand mile non-stop trip, flying about six thousand feet high, traveling close to five hundred miles an hour. This wasn't something to be playing around with.

They bolted the side of the plane back in place, and the engines were started again. Then the captain's voice came on the intercom, saying, "Sorry for the delay. We had a bad air compressor that was replaced. We could have gone on without it because we have two compressors on board, and one is all we really need. I felt better that we had the two."

I still have my opinion as to the mechanics' qualifications as first-class mechanics. But, off we went: next stop Los Angeles, California. In Los Angeles I was going to change planes and go on to Hawaii. I was scheduled to take a day or two to rest in Hawaii. I liked the idea, but I wasn't really tired.

I left California at about seven in the evening on a United Airlines jet. It was a four-engine plane. I think that the regulations for transoceanic flight required a four engine airplane. It was a nice, smooth ride. I always requested a window seat. I like to look at the things below. They seem so small. The only things I saw this night were the lights on a ship every once in a while.

We arrived in Hawaii in a little over seven hours. I took a cab to the Hawaiian Village Hotel where I had reservations. It was located on the famous Waikiki Beach. It was late, and I was a little tired, so I went straight to bed.

I was up bright and early the next morning, ready to do some exploring of the island. I walked to a shopping center close by. There I went into a variety store. They had a long dining counter or bar. People from all the far eastern countries were standing at the bar eating. I eased up close to see what they were eating. The way they were putting the food down, it must have been good, I thought.

I worked myself into a spot at the counter. A waiter asked me what I wanted, and I told him I'd have what everyone else was eating. He set a big plate of steaming brown food in front of me. I asked for a fork. Everyone else was eating with sticks. I took a big bite, chewed a little, got a napkin and spat out the food into it trying as best I could not to let anyone see me. As far as I could make out, what I had ordered was boiled cabbage with lots and lots of some kind of sauce on it. It did the trick; I wasn't hungry anymore.

I went off to do some more looking around. I took a cruise boat to Pearl Harbor to see a ship that was sunk during the bombing of the harbor by the Japanese. The remains of the crew were still aboard the ship. The ship was now a memorial shrine.

I next headed to that famous beach, Waikiki. I thought it wasn't any different from any other beach that I had seen, but it was how the people on the beach were dressed that made it different. There must have been a shortage of cloth for making bathing suits in Hawaii. I didn't visit Diamond Head, but I could see it from my hotel balcony.

The next leg of my trip was to the Fiji Islands. My airplane was a Pan American Airlines super-jet. We would be flying at night. Again, you could see the ship lights and also lights on many small islands in the Pacific Ocean. We arrived in Nandy, Fiji, about midnight. A fleet of cars took us through cane patches and fields for several miles to what they called a hotel. It was a group of one-room buildings, each with a bed, a toilet, and a wash basin. I was tired and went to sleep really quickly.

The next morning I was awakened by knocks on the door. I looked out the window and saw men and women everywhere all dressed the same in skirts or something like that. I washed up, got dressed, and went to what they called a restaurant. It was a thatched roof building with no walls. I ordered eggs and sausage. The eggs were edible, but the sausage wasn't. It was a big link of meat not cooked too well. It was hard to tell what it was made of, so I left it for someone else to eat.

Soon a small airplane arrived from New Zealand. I think it was called an electro-turbo jet. The New Zealand Air Transport was three of these planes. They were more or less shuttle planes from the larger airports. The big jets couldn't land in New Zealand, so they picked up passengers at the larger airfields and took them to New Zealand.

When we left the end of the runway, we were out over the ocean. The runway was just long enough to get airborne. It was a beautiful day, and I could see the many islands of the South Pacific. I noticed that sometimes we were higher above the water than at other times. A steward said that they had no planned flight path and could fly any pattern they chose.

I had a movie camera and was taking pictures of the islands and ships. Only three other people were in the first class section. The captain joined us and pointed out important landmarks. He indicated an island and told us that it belonged to Zane Grey. He said that the famous author came here to write his books. I was leaning against the window taking pictures, and the captain asked if I would like to get a closer look. I said I would. He left and went back to the cockpit, and all at once the plane made a deep dive and circled the island and then went what felt like straight up. I quit taking pictures.

When we arrived in Auckland, there was a Maori driver waiting for me. He loaded my baggage in his car and talked to the customs officers. They waved me through without checking anything. Sandy (the driver's name) had everything under control.

We left the airport for the hundred-mile drive to the Tasman Pulp and Paper Mill. It was located near a very small town called Kawerau at the foot of an inactive volcano called Mt. Edgecombe. I would be staying in Bowater's guest house. I had what they called the "management suite." It was consisted of a bedroom, a full bath, and a large sitting room complete with a balcony. They gave me a new car for transportation. It was an English car similar to our Chevrolet called a Vauxhall.

I had never been treated this royally in my whole life, and I hardly knew how to act. I got wise really quickly, though. It seems that the English look up to someone whom they judge to be important, and they considered me an important person. They asked what time I would be getting up in the mornings. I told them six o'clock A.M.

The next morning at six A.M. sharp there was a knock on my door, and then the door opened and a woman came in carrying a tray. She told me that this was my morning tea. She set the tray down beside the bed and asked if I needed anything. After that I went to the guest house dining room for breakfast. A waiter asked what I would like, and I ordered a couple of eggs, some bacon, toast, and, oh yes, some coffee. I said the tea didn't start my day too well. After breakfast they asked what I would like for lunch.

"I have a choice?" I said.

"We were given orders to prepare anything that you want," I was told.

I wasn't about to let a good thing go, so I said, "How about lamb chops with a couple of vegetables?"

Next I went off for the first day of work with my new "Kiwi" friends. *So far, so good. Don't mess up Charlie,* I told myself.

A Canadian engineer from General Electric was waiting for me at the mill. He had been there for over a year and informed me that he was leaving the next day. I was his replacement. He spent the bigger part of the day showing me around and introducing me to the department heads. We also took a morning tea-time and an evening tea-time. Drinking tea is a way of life for the English.

Once on my own, I began looking things over. Everything was in good shape. They had done a very good job. I asked for an electrician to be my helper. They gave me a young man in his middle twenties named of Keith Singleton. He was a very qualified electrician. He was probably smarter than me, but he would never find that out. I was the expert as far as everyone at the mill knew, and I wasn't about to give up my status. I taught Keith how to record the various outputs on the paper machine drive amplifiers and how to interpret the results of the readings. He did the read-outs regularly each day and at other times if we were experiencing a variation in speeds. He was really good.

At this time, television reception wasn't very good in the valley where we were. Keith confided in me what he and another fellow had done to improve the TV picture quality. They got a car generator, some batteries, and various electronic parts. Then they made a windmill and set it up on the volcanic Mt. Edgecombe. The windmill turned the generator, and the generator charged the batteries that powered the amplifier they had built. They put up an antenna that received the weak signal, amplified it, and sent it to the townspeople in the valley. They were getting pretty good quality TV by the time I left to come home. The government located their station and was going to destroy it, but the local people hollered so loud that the government officials gave Keith permission to operate the station until they could send a stronger signal. I mention this to point out how smart my helper was. He made my job a lot easier.

After about two months, everything was going very smoothly. I could leave the mill some and explore the island. It was a beautiful place. A couple of the men at the plant, the paper machine superintendent and the maintenance manager, took me night deer hunting in the outback bush country. We would spot deer with a light and shoot them. We took only the tenderloin and left the rest of the carcass for the wild hogs. The entire deer would be eaten by them within two hours.

I had an accident on one trip. I put my nose too close to the scope on the gun, and when I fired it the recoil caused the scope to cut the bridge of my nose. The town had two medical doctors. One doctor was always on duty, so the next morning I took a seat in the doctor's office and waited my turn. No appointment was necessary. Like England, New Zealand had a "socialized" medical system.

Soon my turn came, and I went in to see the doctor. Before me sat a chubby man wearing short pants and a shirt that had food all over the front of it. He was my doctor. He put a towel over my eyes, sprayed something over the cut, and said, "That's it. I'm done."

"Aren't you going to stitch it up so there won't be a scar?" I inquired.

"Are you married?" he asked.

"Yes," I said.

"Then it doesn't matter if you have a scar. Next!" he hollered.

I had a first-aid kit that I brought with me. I used nail clippers and made some strips from tape. I scrubbed the cut really well with soap and pulled the cut together by putting the strips across the cut. I left the tape strips on until the wound healed.

I was invited to a brunch one Sunday, and the doctor happened to be there. He was drinking pretty heavily, and I struck up a conversation with him. I asked where he was working before coming to Kawerau. He said he had been doctoring all over Burma, mostly traveling by train from village to village. I asked if he ever had people die while working on them; he said many had. I asked him what he would do with them. He said he'd throw them off the train into the jungle and let the animals take care of them. I'm sure glad I never got sick while I was in Kawerau.

I had many unusual experiences while in New Zealand. I visited the "hot fields" where the ground erupts steam and hot water created by the deep volcanic activity occurring on the North Island. The natural hot water is so plentiful that the paper mill has a geothermal farm, a group of wells that supply steam for the mill. The mill had one geothermally driven turbine that generated part of the electrical power for the mill. I went bathing in one of the larger lakes that were heated from the underground volcanic activity. The closer you got to the center, the hotter it got.

Another thing I'll always remember is the sheep. They said that there were more sheep in New Zealand than there were people. I can believe this. I was out one Sunday evening when all of a sudden there were thousands of sheep coming down the road. I stopped the car to let them pass, and it seemed like an hour before the last sheep went by. A man on a horse rode at the back of the herd. He had several dogs that kept the sheep together. This was a common thing, I was told. The sheep have the right-of-way on the roads when they are being taken from one pasture to another. These pastures were called paddocks.

I also had one of the old native Maori catch a wallaby for me. This animal is something like a miniature kangaroo. I intended to bring it back with me when I returned home. I had a friend keep it for me. One day his maid let it out of the closed-in porch where he was keeping it, and it got away. I didn't have time to go catch another. I also tried to catch a mynah bird. The natives said you could teach them to talk. I didn't have any luck with this project either.

One thing that was something new to me was the local pub. It was very large, and most of the people in the town would gather there every evening for fellowship and beer. The beer was delivered in tank trucks like our gasoline is transported. They even stored it in underground tanks. The bartenders used a hose and nozzle to serve out the beer into large pitchers, just like putting gas in your car tank. Gathering at the pub made the locals' day, I am told.

Well, the time for me to return home came. Arrangements were made for me to ride a small plane that transported passengers to the airport in Auckland. A taxi picked me up and took me to a large grassy field. The taxi driver told me that an airplane would land and pick me up, and then he left. Soon I heard a plane. I watched it, thinking it would land to get me, but it just kept going. It finally turned and came back and landed. I got on, and the pilot said that he had forgotten that I was to be picked up. Shortly, we were at the Auckland Airport. The same man who had met me when I first arrived in New Zealand met me and took me to one of the hotels in Auckland. My plane back to the Fiji islands was not leaving until six o'clock that evening. I was to rest until near departure time, and then he would come and take me back to the airport to catch my plane.

By about six P.M., I was on my way to Nandy. It was dark, so I couldn't see anything below except the lights on a ship or an island. I arrived in Nandy around midnight. This time, I went directly from the smaller plane to a large TWA jet which would take me to Hawaii. I stopped over for one day in Hawaii before going on to Tennessee.

Marie and the boys met me at the Chattanooga Airport. They seemed glad to see me, and I sure was glad to be home once again. Gary and Dean were disappointed that I hadn't brought back the wallaby. I rested up for a week at home before returning to my job at Bowater in Calhoun.

When I got back to work, everything seemed the same as before. The secretary came to my office and said that Lowell Culbertson, our vice-president and mill manager, wanted me to come to his office. I went right away.

"Charlie," he said, "the report that we get from the people at Tasman is that you helped them very much. I want to give you something to show our appreciation for doing a good job."

He handed me a check. I looked at it, and it was for one thousand dollars. I said that this wasn't necessary but that I could always use more money. I thanked him and went back to the Engineering Office.

Everything was back to normal really quickly. I needed something to keep me busy when I was not at the mill. I wanted to try my hand at politics. I decided to run for the office of city commissioner. I submitted all the paper work and was placed on the ballot for the upcoming election.

As the election drew near, I took a week's vacation to do some campaigning. I knocked on thousands of doors and talked to that many people about voting for me. Many promised to vote for me. I didn't think I would get elected because I favored the Democratic Party, and the county and city were mostly made up of Republicans.

Two Republicans, another Democrat, and I were running for the office. My fellow Democrat was a well-known African American named Saint James. He owned and operated a dance hall called "The House of Happy Feet." He was a very nice guy. He and I knew that we didn't have much of a chance to win, so we didn't spend a lot of money on advertising. I had some cards printed, and Saint James didn't spend any money at all. We just had a good time talking to people. My main concern was to not let Saint James beat me. When the voting was done and the ballots were counted, there were no surprises. The candidate who had a lot of influence with the local Christian college and the backing of local church groups was elected. I only got a little over two hundred votes more than Saint James. This was a victory for me.

Later on, I was appointed a member of the Bradley County Election Commission. During my second term on the Commission, I was elected chairman. I did not want to serve another term on the Commission, and I asked to be replaced. I also served on the City Planning Commission for one term. That was the extent of my political career.

I also got involved in many other projects. I built a houseboat using fifty-five gallon oil drums for pontoons. The boat would sleep four. It had a toilet and a gas stove. We didn't use it very much, so I sold it and bought a travel trailer. It would sleep six people and had all the necessities for camping out. We didn't use this very much either, sort of like the houseboat. I sold the trailer, also.

I was a member of the Masonic Lodge at Charleston, Tennessee. I received all the degrees that made me eligible for Shrine membership. I was pretty active in the Shriners for a long time. My Shrine Temple had property on the lake at Soddy Daisy, Tennessee. A member could get a lot for a trailer or a house there without cost other than utilities expenses and membership dues. I chose to build a cabin on a lot there.

I drew plans for my cabin and had them approved by the property board. It would have a bedroom, a living room, and a full basement with kitchen, bath, and recreation room. I pre-fabricated all of the walls and roof trusses for the cabin in my driveway after work each evening. I borrowed a farm hay wagon and loaded the complete house on it and hauled it to the lot on the lake. I had to have someone lay block and pour the basement floor. I did the plumbing, using copper pipe in the concrete floor. The building took me nearly two years to complete. I did all the work myself except the concrete work.

Marie wasn't an away-from-home type of person. She wanted to be in her own familiar bed at home when the sun went down. Here again, the cabin wasn't used as it should have been. Gary and his family used it for about a year while he was attending the University of Tennessee at Chattanooga. His children really enjoyed the beach on the lake-side property. I asked the board about selling the cabin. I was told I could sell to another Shriner, but I was not to make a profit from the sale. I placed a For Sale sign in the yard one Saturday morning, and it was sold before noon that day.

With all my many projects and political adventures behind me, I was ready to slow down and wait for the day I would reach the age of sixty-two and be eligible for retirement.

# RETIRED

It had been thirty-plus years since I came to Bowater. Time sure goes by fast. Although I'd looked forward to retiring, I began to wonder what I would do with all the time I'd have when I left Bowater. There would be no getting out of bed at five every morning for five days a week; no driving to work in all kinds of weather long before daylight.

I had enjoyed my work over the years, taking the bad along with the good, and I actually looked forward to going to my job. It seemed that no two days were the same. I had plenty of work to do with a good group of co-workers. This was the Mill Engineering Department, people helping people. That was what it was all about, and now I was about to leave behind everything that had been a part of my life for over thirty years.

Things started to happen the last week I was at work. I came home one evening, and Marie informed me that we were going out to eat with our friends the Brewers. We did this often, so I didn't give it much thought. I bathed and got dressed. It was a little strange that the clothes I was to wear were lying on the bed when I came out of the bath. They were dressier than what I usually wore when going out to dinner. I didn't argue about the change of dress. I put on the clothes that were laid out for me and was ready when Dick and Marylyn Brewer arrived.

Dick said that he would drive his car. We usually went to Chattanooga when we went out to eat, but we were taking a different route this time. When I questioned him about it, he said he thought he'd go a different way this time. Soon I began to get suspicious. We were pulling into the Elks Lodge parking lot. We had eaten there before as a guest of a member, but neither Dick nor I were members of the Lodge. We parked and went in.

This is where I got the surprise of my life. This large meeting room was decorated with all kinds of signs and pictures. Some were serious and some were funny. And, also, eighty-seven of my co-workers and friends were there. They were going to "roast" me. That they did and really good at that. They had also hired a good-looking belly dancer. I guess the reason that I say good-looking is that she had left most of her clothes in Chattanooga. I can say truly that she was a good entertainer, and all of her attention was on me.

The crowd enjoyed the show with me at front and center more than I did. Ten or twelve speakers took the stand to tell all the things I had done wrong or funny over the past years (nothing good). It was a big surprise and to me a highlight of my many years working with these people. I didn't deserve this kind of farewell.

On the following Monday my employment at Bowater was officially over. This was not exactly so, however. Soon, I was asked if I would do some special projects for Bowater. They wanted me to work as a consultant. They rented me an office in Cleveland. I would get the details of their requirements from Engineering and do all the work in Cleveland. The agreement was that I would only work until

I earned the limit allowable by Social Security before they began reducing my benefits.

I didn't let this work interfere with my golfing. I had played a little golf before retiring, but I got into it pretty heavily now. I was a member of the Waterville Golf Club, and I joined in a foursome made up of other retirees. We were at the number one tee every morning at eight o'clock, Monday through Friday, if the weather was half decent. I worked at home during the afternoon. I also did my Bowater consulting work in the afternoons and on bad weather days. In this way, I managed to keep things going.

Marie and I were the only ones at home now. The boys had moved away and had families of their own. We started planning on going to Florida for the winter months. We would be warm there, and I could get in some golfing. We began to look for someplace that was affordable and in a good location. We found a place in Winter Haven, Florida. The price was right. The cabins on Lake Ida were old but clean and comfortable. Also, we got daily maid service, which Marie liked. We leased the cabin only for one month just to see if we would like Florida living.

The fishing was good, but the golfing wasn't too good. The local course was only a par three. I played once or twice a week. Marie and I enjoyed ourselves, I guess, the most we had since we were married. We took long walks and visited the shopping centers together. This was the most time we had spent together alone in our married life. We were always busy earlier in our married life. Marie took care of the house and the boys; I spent most of my time at Bowater. Retirement was great so far.

Marie had a sister who lived at Frost Proof. This was about thirty miles south of Winter Haven. We visited her and her husband several times, and they came to see us, also, at Winter Haven. Marie liked this. Marie's sister, Pansy, and her husband, Lewin, had a good friend who had several citrus groves. He grew oranges, grapefruits, tangerines, and some other tropical fruits. We became acquainted with him, and he let us pick all the fruit we wanted to bring back to Tennessee. This was great, and we brought back all we could fit into our car.

I worked for Bowater part time the first summer after retirement. This gave us some extra money for our expenses for a winter stay in Florida. We decided to try somewhere else besides Winter Haven for our second winter. We had friends who were staying at New Smyrna Beach, so we found a condominium there. We were on the eighth floor of the condo on the ocean side, and we had a good view of everything that took place on the beach and on the ocean. We could watch the fishing boats and shrimp boats about every night.

We were only about twenty miles from Cape Canaveral Space Center, and NASA was getting ready to launch a space flight. We could see the launch area from our balcony, but we decided to drive down and get a closer view of the launch. It was really cold the morning we went. I had binoculars and could see ice on the space shuttle. We heard that the lift-off was postponed until the next day. We had planned to watch it from our balcony, but it being still pretty cold, we decided to drive down again for a closer look.

They started the countdown, and there was a lift-off. The shuttle wasn't too high when all of a sudden it exploded. Pieces went in all directions. The voice on the public address speakers went silent. Everyone watching became silent, too. We went to the car, and I don't think we spoke more than a dozen words all the way to the condo. We were sad. All the crew of the spacecraft were killed instantly.

There wasn't a good golf course at New Smyrna, so I did a lot of fishing in the Intracostal Waterway and the Indian River. The trout fishing was good. I dressed the trout I caught and had the cook at a local seafood restaurant cook them for us. He also gave us some hush puppies.

We met an elderly couple from New Jersey who were in the condo next to us. The man had his car shipped from New Jersey to Florida by Amtrak. He wanted me to drive and take them places. They had spent the previous winter at a place in Orlando that they recommended. They gave us phone numbers to call to make arrangements to stay there. We did this the next fall as we were making preparations to go for the winter.

    This group of condos was very nice. It had been built by General Electric on a five-hundred-acre tract of land. It had one of the top golf courses in Florida for its residents. The complex had security guards at its entrance gate twenty-four hours a day. It was very private. The place was called Ventura. Living here, we were close to many the amusement parks such as Disney World, Universal Studios, Sea World and lots of smaller ones. There were three large shopping centers nearby. Marie liked this. There were many top-notch golf courses, and good restaurants. There was also a good church that we attended, the First Baptist Church of Orlando. Their pastor, Jim Henry, was from Nashville, Tennessee.

    Arnold Palmer's Bay Hill was close by. One of its residents was Victor Sutton, the CEO at Bowater and my old boss. He was the one who sent me to New Zealand. He heard that I was in Orlando at Ventura, got my phone number from the office, and called me. He invited me to come to Bay Hill and play a round of golf with him. Of course I accepted. He said he would call me when he got a tee time.

    He called a few days later. There was a large shopping center on the way to Bay Hill. This was perfect: I took Marie there to go shopping, and I would pick her up on my way back after golfing. When I arrived, Vic was ready. His house was on the golf course. He had his own golf cart. We went to the club house, and the Florida rains started to come down. We waited for a long time and finally gave up on golf and settled for a sandwich and soup at the club-house restaurant. He said he would call again sometime for golfing.

    He drove me around pointing out where some famous golfers such as Payne Stewart lived. I asked where Arnold Palmer lived, and he pointed out his condo. All the homes at Bay Hill were million-dollar homes. I was thinking that Arnold would have the best one, but it turned out that he had the smallest.

We had three great winters at Ventura. We had our children and close friends visit us there. Our place would sleep six people. It was very nice when we had visitors. We would take them to Disney World and other attractions. We saw all these places at least five times.

The following winter at Ventura was somewhat different for me. I didn't play very much golf. Before, I usually played every day, but not this winter. When Marie asked why, I told her I didn't feel too well. I didn't have any energy. I just felt tired all the time. I had been seeing a doctor in Cleveland about passing blood every time that I used the toilet. I had numerous x-rays taken of my bowels and the diagnosis was always the same: bleeding hemorrhoids.

We returned to Cleveland the last of March, and I went to the Veterans Administration out-patient clinic in Chattanooga. They assigned me to a retired Army doctor named Gekeyes. He examined me and confirmed that I was passing blood. He also said that it wasn't from hemorrhoids. I was in and out of the radiology department all day long. At about three o'clock that afternoon, Doctor Gekeyes had me to come back to his office.

"I have bad news," he said. "You have cancer of the colon. I'm sending you to the VA hospital in Nashville. The cancer needs to be removed as soon as possible."

I told him that I had insurance that would pay for my medical expenses, and I had rather have the surgery done in Cleveland. He said that I could take all the pictures and other test results from the VA clinic and give them to the surgeon who would do the surgery. Having them would save time since the tests wouldn't have to be redone.

Sarah, Dean's daughter, was spending the summer with us. I had taken her and Marie to the shopping mall to stay while I was at the VA clinic. I was to pick them up on my way back home. We thought I would be gone only a couple of hours instead of all day. I went by for them. They were tired from waiting so long. I told them the news. Everyone was silent not wanting to talk about what was going to happen. Marie called Dean and told him the news. He was in the Army and stationed in Virginia at the time. He left immediately to come and take Sarah home.

I went to my gastroenterologist in Cleveland. He wanted to take a look by doing a colonoscopy before surgery. He told me to be at his office at seven the next morning. I was on time, and he was waiting. I asked to be placed so I could see the monitor screen while he did the endoscopic examination. I was able to see the cancerous spot. It looked like a rose with blood oozing from its center. After the procedure he told that whatever it was it had to be removed because it had my colon blocked. He had taken biopsies to see if it was cancer. He recommended Dr. James Knabb as the one to do the surgery.

I went to Dr. Knabb's office, and he sent me to have CAT scan done to use when doing the surgery. He scheduled the surgery for two days later at Bradley Memorial Hospital. The hospital was only two blocks from our house which would be convenient. Marie wouldn't have to travel far to visit. I was going to be in the hospital for two weeks.

Dr. Knabb did the surgery and came by to talk with me after I was awake. He had removed thirteen inches of my colon. He said that he was pretty sure that he got all of the infected area but wanted me to go to a cancer doctor once I was home and able to get around.

I was home in about two weeks. A week later I went to Doctor Dugan, the cancer doctor. After lots of tests, he said there was no sign of further cancer. He also said that as a precautionary measure, it would be wise to take radiation treatments, just to be sure. I asked what the odds of the cancer coming back were if I didn't take the treatments. He said that it would be ninety percent likely to recur without radiation treatment and ninety percent likely *not* to recur with radiation. I asked when he wanted to start the treatments, and he told me as soon as possible.

My stomach was tattooed for focusing the radiation, and the treatments began. I was to take one treatment every day Monday through Friday with no treatments on Saturday and Sunday. They did bother me some, but I kept moving about to keep my mind off feeling bad.

The treatments were soon over, and I was back to doing work for Bowater. That year we went back to Orlando and had a great winter. I felt great. I played lots of golf and spent lots of time in the malls with Marie. Everything was back to normal with our retirement.

That was the last winter that we went to Florida for an extended stay. We became more involved around the house. Marie had her flowers. I had a garden along with the yard work and some golfing. I also bought some woodworking tools and began making some small pieces of furniture for our house and for the children. I made a few clocks, and to my surprise there was a market for them.

I made mostly school clocks. I cut out the outline of the state that the school was located in, sanded the wood, and trimmed the edges with the school's colors. I then added whatever the customer wanted for the face along with hour numbers. After that I poured a mixture of resin and hardener over the entire clock. After setting for ten hours, the front had a glass-like covering. I then added the movement and hands.

There were special occasions when I had to make several hundred clocks of the same design. Once, when the University of Tennessee removed the artificial turf from their playing field and planted grass, I used the old turf on my clocks. I had a friend who was the engineer in charge of the turf replacement project. He gave me several pieces of the old turf. I washed it and cut small pieces in the shape of a football to go on the clocks. I also showed the dates that the turf was installed and removed. There was a great demand for these clocks from the many UT fans.

The biggest demand for these University of Tennessee clocks came the year UT won the national championship. I estimate that I made somewhere around a thousand clocks to commemorate this. I had orders from everywhere. If I was lucky, I could make six clocks every twenty-four hours—three in the early morning and three in the afternoon. Marie wanted me to make lots of them because I gave her all the money that I earned selling them. She used it for a few things around the house, but most of it went toward something for the grandchildren. She was happy, and I was happy because this gave me something to do to keep me busy.

At one time I had to teach Dean clock making so he could help me keep up with the demand. This gave him some extra money, also. He made quite a few, but he soon tired of the time-consuming process, and he called it quits. I also made clocks representing different schools in other states for the Hobby Lobby shop at the Hamilton Mall shopping center in Chattanooga.

I finally had to stop making clocks. I had stopped making a garden, and I didn't play very much golf. It seemed the work was increasing. I didn't want to admit that it was me just getting older and slower.

Marie and I went on a few short trips and kept busy around the house, enjoying our senior years. All of a sudden, our lifestyle took a change. I came home from the grocery store early on the morning of October twenty-first, 2002, and found Marie sick. She had all the symptoms of a heart attack. I recognized what was happening and rushed her to the emergency room at the hospital. Sure enough, she was having a heart attack. After monitoring her over night and taking heart examination, pictures the doctors found that the arteries going to her heart were blocked.

There was only one thing to do: by-pass surgery. Her cardiologist called Memorial Hospital in Chattanooga and made arrangements for surgery. She was taken by ambulance to Memorial where the surgery was to be done the next morning, October twenty-fourth, 2002.

Everything went smoothly. They did four by-passes on her heart. The surgeon called Dean and me to tell us about the surgery. He said that he noticed something odd about her lungs. The outside of her lungs was rough like sandpaper. He had a lung specialist take a look and get a sample to check for cancer. We would know the results of the test the next day. The lung doctor came by Marie's hospital room and said that the results were good. There was no sign of cancer. Further tests were recommended after she recovered from the heart surgery.

She did very well and was soon up and about working with her flowers. She said she felt really well. We went to the lung doctor in Cleveland who the hospital had recommended, a Dr. Marcum. After many tests (a sleep test, a nuclear test, a breathing test, and others), he ordered her to be on oxygen at night. This was a big blow to Marie and me. The doctor said she had fibrosis of the lungs. No one knew what caused this, and there was no treatment for it; only oxygen would help. She managed to keep her disease secret from her brothers and sisters and the neighbors for nearly two years.

For the last six months of her life, Marie suffered from a lack of oxygen, even with the assistance of her breathing apparatus. She kept getting weaker and suffered a rapid loss of weight even when she was eating well. I tried many times to get her to go back to the doctor to get some other treatment, but she wouldn't go.

Dean and Soon came to spend the night on November fifth, 2004. As soon as Dean saw his mother on the couch he said, "Mother, you need to be in the hospital."

"I'll go see a doctor Monday," she said. (This was a Friday evening.)

Dean picked up the phone and called our family doctor. He said for us to take her to the hospital emergency room. I got her into the car, and they were waiting for us outside the emergency room when we arrived. After some time, they got her stabilized and said she would have to stay that night for observation. She slept well that night.

I was up to her room at six A.M. the next morning. I helped her do her make up, and I combed her hair. She ate a good breakfast. During the day, we sat and watched television. We watched a University of Tennessee football game that evening. She said that she was feeling good. She asked me to go get her a chocolate candy bar. She said she wasn't supposed to eat chocolate but craved it. I stayed with Marie in the hospital until bed time each day for several days. We talked and watched TV. Tuesday night she wanted to go to sleep early. The nurse gave her a sleeping pill, and I went home. On Wednesday morning she didn't want to eat. I helped her with her hair and make up, and she wanted to sleep.

Dean and Gary were there on Wednesday after the doctor came by. They said that they were going back to their homes but would be back soon. I didn't give this much thought. She slept most of the day, and I stayed with her. I could sense that something unusual was happening. On Monday after entering the hospital Marie had asked me to go home and get her living will and give it to the doctor. I had tried to put it off, but she told me this couldn't wait, that it had to be done now. I had gone home and brought it back and given it to the nurse.

On Thursday morning I was at the hospital at six A.M. I was combing her hair when the nurse called me out into the hallway. She said, "I suppose you know that your wife is dying."

I said, "No, I don't."

"The doctor told your sons yesterday."

This was a shock to me. This explained the sudden trips home that the children had taken. They went to get dress clothing for their mother's funeral.

After I got Marie comfortable, I walked a little ways from the hospital to her lung doctor's office. I asked his nurse if he would talk with me. After a minute she informed me that he didn't have time for me. I wanted to know about Marie's condition. I will never forget this rudeness. If ever I need a lung doctor, I sure don't want this one.

Marie was in and out of sleep all day. At one time, she said to me, "You know, I don't see how I could have got along all these years without you."

This broke my heart because she had never said anything like this before. I do believe that sometimes before dying, a person somehow knows that he or she is dying.

On November twelfth, 2004, the hospital moved Marie to a private room about an hour before she died. We had tried to get a private room for her all week; they had said there wasn't one available. Dean was counting the time between her breaths now. I put my hand under the blanket and took her hand. She opened her eyes and gave a deep breath, and then she was gone.

Here came all the nurses and the doctor who wouldn't talk to me. He did the things that they do before pronouncing a person dead. He turned to me and said, "I'm sorry I didn't talk with you this morning."

I never gave him an answer.

The nurse wanted to know which funeral home I wanted her to call. I told her to call Buckner Funeral Home. Marie and I had made all the arrangements for our burial several years earlier. She had picked out her casket and mine, also. Her request had been to be buried back in North Carolina in the same graveyard where her brothers and sisters were buried. I had purchased two burial plots in Crawford Cemetery between Canton and Clyde, North Carolina.

She had two funerals—one here in Cleveland and one in North Carolina. Our pastor, Dr. Jay McClusky, conducted both services. He was not only our pastor but also a very good friend. We had baby-sat for him and his wife when they first moved to Cleveland. Marie's good friend, Nancy Paul, sang at the Cleveland service. Dr. Jay led the singing at the service in North Carolina. The Buckner Funeral Home in Cleveland did a wonderful service. Kim Randolph, the owner of the funeral home, drove the hearse to North Carolina himself. He said he wanted to make sure Marie got all the respect she deserved.

I'm all alone now. The boys, Dean and Gary, both fixed up rooms in their homes for me to stay with them. I spent two nights at Dean's and three at Gary's. But, I like to be at my own home where I can do the things that I want to do and not feel like I'm imposing on someone. After all, they have a family to take care of.

Until you experience the things that one goes through as I have, you will never know the sadness of losing someone whom you have been with night and day for nearly sixty years. You never forget the good times or the bad times. It is all a part of life and part of the pleasure of having a family.

The years that I have left in my retirement will not be the same as the ones I had when Marie was alive, I know. I live day by day making the best I can of things. I will carry on with the help of God.

# GRANDCHILDREN

Up to this point I haven't said anything about our grandchildren. Although their story isn't the story of my life, they are playing a very big role in my growing older. On the next few pages I will try to recall a few things that have happened with my grandchildren and me. It seems that the grandchildren in every family are just a little more important than our very own children, or at least it looks that way. I guess the reason for parents to think this way is because we were always with our own children from the day they were born until the day they were married and left home to start their own family. This is the way it was with Marie and me.

Gary and his wife Katsue were the first to present us with a grandchild, a boy, and his name is Geoffrey. A boy was just what I wanted. He began to get spoiled by his grandparents from day one. This never stopped happening with him or any of the other seven that came along in a matter of a very few years. Gary and his wife Katsue presented us with five grandchildren, three boys and two girls. In order of age they are Geoffrey, Amy, George, Alice, and William. Dean and his wife, Soon, gave us three. Again, starting with the oldest, they are Ben, Sarah, and Josh. I didn't give their full Christian names, only the ones that I use when talking or referring to one of them.

I'll try to recall some of the more important things that have happened between them and me. If anyone remembers differently, please excuse my version, as age has a funny way of interpreting memories, and I am no exception to this. From the time that they could be away from their mothers for a long period of time, they were at our house. Here they got whatever they wanted and did about anything they chose to do. This was not the way it was with our boys, they only got about half the attention that the grandchildren received.

Gary's children were the first to get the royal treatment that all grandparents bestow on their grandchildren. It seems that the first one that comes along gets the most attention. This was Geoffrey, Gary's first child. We were keeping him as soon as he could survive on solid food. He was spoiled by his grandma something awful. The next was Amy. She too soon became a part of our second family. Dean was still at home when not in school, but he didn't get the special attention that he once received. It didn't seem to bother him; in fact I think he liked the way things were going. He wasn't watched as closely as he was before the little ones were here, and, in a way, this gave him more freedom to do as he liked.

Gary was in graduate school in Knoxville at the University of Tennessee at the time. Every Friday evening after finishing my work, I would go to Knoxville and bring Geoff and Amy to Cleveland and would take them back on Sunday afternoon. They never wanted to leave. We had to change the pattern of bringing the two at the same time. They were always fussing and fighting with each other thinking that the other one was getting more attention, so they had to alternate weekends.

When George was old enough to come stay, I began to take the boys camping at Cade's Cove in the Great Smoky Mountains National

Park. I bought a tent that would sleep four people. It was kind of comfortable, well, as much as a tent could be. I did all the cooking and cleaning, and they kept me pretty busy from daylight to dark. Seems they were always hungry. They found friends to play and hike with, and I would ride them around the Cove road that they called the "loop." This was a twelve-mile, one-way scenic road passing the old churches and other buildings that were left behind from the people who lived in the Cove before the government took the land and made it a national park. Cade's Cove was a big part of the history of the settlement of this country. The buildings are well kept up, and they are very big tourist attraction.

Soon, Dean was married and starting a family of his own. Ben was the first of the three children that he and Soon had. He didn't get carried away like Gary, who gave us five grandchildren. He said three, and that's it. There was Ben, then Sarah, and along came Josh. We never had the chance to have Dean's children with us very often because he made the Army his choice of work, and he was always moving and never lived close enough for us to keep his children. As they grew older, he would bring them to our house sometimes.

I did get to take Ben to Cade's Cove for a few days of camping out. He seemed to enjoy himself, especially at night. After it became dark we would get our flashlights and go to the picnic area to look for the animals that were feeding from the garbage cans. We saw several bear and lots and lots of skunks. We made sure to keep our distance from the skunks and that bear. We did this every night, and so did lots of other people who were camping there.

One day I got back from the trip around the loop, and there was something exciting going on. Ben, George, Geoff and some other boys about their age had chased two young bear cubs that had become separated from their mother up a tree. I made them all get away from the cubs before the mother bear came back. She could have hurt them; bear are very protective of their cubs.

When Dean was stationed in the Netherlands and Ben was seven years old, Dean bought him a round-trip airplane ticket so that he could come spend the summer with us. This was great because we didn't get to see Dean's children very often. Geoff was staying with us so he could finish his senior year at Cleveland High School, and Gary was in Japan at that time. We met Ben at the airport and from that day until he was to go home he and Geoff were inseparable. When Geoff wasn't at work, they had a great time together. Ben and Geoff went to Six Flags amusement park in Georgia one day. Geoff's old car had a habit of getting vapor locked, and it had to sit a few minutes for the carburetor to cool before it would start. Ben gave Geoff a rough time over this.

When it was time for Ben to go back to the Netherlands, I took him to the airport in Atlanta so he wouldn't have to change planes. When we checked in at the airport, the airlines clerk said that his reservations were for the next day, but Ben's ticket said they were for this day. After a lot of checking they said they had made a mistake and that they would make room for him. So, Ben left that day even though he wanted to come back to Cleveland and go the next day. The clerk put an identification tag around Ben's neck and off he went. I learned later that he sat in the section reserved for the airline personnel. He made it home okay. We sure missed him; he kept us busy all the time he wasn't sleeping.

Ben and all the other seven are grown up and out on their own now. I am thankful that they still like to come to our house. Most of them are too far away to visit often. Ben comes and spends the weekend with me very often, as he is in graduate school in Knoxville. I look forward to his visits. He too will soon be relocating, and then the visits from my grandchildren will be few and far between.

This is only a small part of all the things that took place with our grandchildren. I write this to let the future generations know that they were a great part of my life, and I shall never forget them. Everyone's grandchildren are just a little better in their sight than everybody else's grandchildren. I also think this way.

# LIVING ALONE

Here I am, all alone, after sixty years of being with someone, most of the time knowing that there would be someone else at home when I was there. All of a sudden, it's not that way anymore. This is my situation since Marie died; I am all alone.

Dean spent several days with me after Marie's funeral, and I told him, "I can get along okay. I've got to get myself together and carry on. I can do it by myself."

After getting all the business taken care of that comes with someone dying, I started making a list of the things that needed doing during the following weeks: washing clothes, mopping the kitchen, sweeping the garage, and all the other things that were done around the house regularly. I checked each thing off as I completed it. This seemed to work pretty well. I then began some remodeling projects around the house that were put off because of Marie's sickness.

First I contacted the Goodwill Store and asked if they would take the upright freezer that we quit using several years ago. We didn't need a lot of food since there were only two people in the family. The boys had moved out a long time ago. Goodwill set a date for when they would pick up the freezer. After it was gone, I had a cabinet shop come by and get measurements for building a pantry in the place where the freezer was. After it was installed, Dean came and painted it for me. Then Soon came and did all the moving of pots and pans. She did a great job. After that it took me several weeks to locate what I needed when cooking.

The next job that I had planned on doing but had put off because of Marie's being sick was remodeling the bathrooms. I started the bigger job first. One of the bathrooms needed a new vanity and new sink with all new fixtures. I also installed new lighting and a new mirror. Next, I built a cabinet with shelves for towels and wash cloths. When the job was completed it looked like a different room. I was proud of this make-over.

Next, I started on what we called the big bathroom. There wasn't as much to do here as in the other bath. I replaced the lighting and the fixtures on the sink. I also built a cabinet for towels. This was all that needed to be done in this room.

Tim, the owner of the sports store at the Hamilton Mall in Chattanooga asked me if I would make him some clocks for a new store that he was opening at the North Gate Mall. I agreed to make him twelve clocks: four University of Tennessee clocks, four University of Georgia clocks, and four University of Alabama clocks. I made them, and when I took them to his store at the Hamilton Mall I told him I wouldn't be able to make him any more. I hated to tell him this because he was a very good customer. Over the years he had bought nearly all the clocks that I took to him.

Recently, I have made several mantle clocks as gifts. I also made many banana trees and bird boxes that I gave away. These I made when I had slack time. I do these things to keep myself busy. I find that things are lots better for me if I keep my mind on something other than myself.

My neighbor saw the changes I had made to my bathrooms, and he asked if I would help him do one of his baths. I agreed to help. Helping him would keep me busy during my difficult time of getting used to living alone. His job required more work than I had done on my bathrooms. I not only replaced a mirror and the lighting along with a new vanity and sink, but I had to replace the plumbing under the sink also. Anyway, I got the job completed.

During the first year it was pretty lonesome during the winter months. I spent the bad days in the house reading, and on the warmer days I did some kind of wood-working project—anything to keep busy.

Spring soon arrived, and I began working in the flower beds getting them ready for new flowers as soon as the weather warmed up and it stopped frosting. I promised myself several years ago that I would dig up all the flowers and plant grass. Having a pretty flower bed involves a lot of work. I couldn't make myself do this, though, as we have had lots of flowers as far back as I can remember. I went to the FFA department at Bradley High School and bought 240 flower plants to set out. They were all kinds of colors, and they bloomed all summer long.

Little did I think that I would ever have my abdomen cut open again after the cancer surgery several years ago, but it was about to happen again. I was having some trouble with my bowels, but I thought it would get well on its own. One Friday in April 2004, my intestines completely blocked up. The only thing that would help was to have Dr. Knabb do surgery. He would have to do some bypasses in my colon. He did the surgery, and everything was fine after two weeks in the hospital. I came home, and Soon spent my first week at home with me. Katsue spent the following week with me. I was able to make it on my own after two weeks of nursing by my daughters-in-law. I began to eat anything I wanted, and I also began to gain weight. I was soon above one hundred and eighty pounds; this was the most I had ever weighed. My usual weight had been between 150 and 160 pounds.

It has been three years since the bypasses, and now I am having some blockage like before. My gastrointestinal doctor asked me if I would have surgery again. I answered that if it was certain that more surgery would help me so I could once again eat solid food, I might consider doing it again; but I also said that because I was nearly 85 years old, I didn't recover as easily as younger people. He explained that I was in very good condition mentally and physically for my age. He said some people were old at 50 or 60 years old and that others weren't old even at 70 or 80 years old. I think he was trying to make me feel younger than I am. I decided to just take one day at a time and see what happens.

While reading the newspaper, I saw the schedule of activities at the Senior Center. They had bridge games every Tuesday afternoon. I hadn't played any bridge for over forty years, but I began to think playing bridge would get me away from the house one day every week. This would also exercise my mind. I made a trip to the Center and joined the bridge club.

I got the phone number of the bridge club director, and I called and asked if I could start playing bridge with the club. He told me that I could begin the next Tuesday. There was a problem though; I didn't have a partner. The director, Jeep Tullos, said that I needn't worry because he'd find me a partner. My first partner was Doctor Bower's wife. She was a very good player and also very understanding and patient with me. I was very nervous sitting in a room with about sixty seasoned players, but they made me feel welcome and made me a part of the club.

I have a regular bridge partner now. He isn't the best bridge player, but he is the biggest player. He is 6 feet 8 inches tall and weighs about 370 pounds. He is retired from Sonic Restaurants where he was a co-owner. We are not the best players, but we are not the worst players either. We finish $2^{nd}$ or close to $2^{nd}$ once in a while. Sometimes we are last, but not very often. He only wants to play once a week.

I have played in several tournaments and sometimes play at the Country Club at their Saturday games. The biggest tournament I have been in was a by-invitation-only tournament held at the Hardwick Farms. This was a three-day affair, Thursday thru Saturday. We played twenty-seven games in the afternoon and the same number of games that night each day on Thursday and Friday. On Saturday a special game called a "Swiss game" was held. I had never even heard of this, but I got thru it okay. There was a big dinner on Saturday evening as well as dancing in a large tent with a hardwood floor. There was a dance band for the music and entertainment. I enjoyed the meal but didn't do any dancing, although I like to dance, or I did when I was younger. One reason I didn't dance was that I didn't have a partner (lady) to dance with.

My regular bridge partner didn't play in this tournament, as he was on vacation in Florida. I played with a retired CPA whose name is Warren Mitchell. He is a top-notch player and very serious. I can't get too serious about the game. I enjoy myself, and I have a good time because life is too short to worry if things don't turn out the way you want them to. I'm looking forward to the big tournament next year at the Farm; that is, if I am invited. There were over 100 players at this year's tournament and about 150 people attended party afterwards. They were from all over the country: Texas, Georgia, Virginia, Tennessee, and other places, I'm sure.

I make a trip to North Carolina several times a year to take flowers to Marie's grave. Dean usually takes me, as I don't drive long trips anymore because my eyesight is failing. I think my driving is still good; it's only that I don't trust my vision. On the last trip Dean, Soon, and I spent a night with my brother T.J. He wants us to spend the night on our next trip. We like to talk about the past.

On the next trip I want to visit Conrad Wines. He is my old well-digging buddy from back in the '30s. He has moved back to the old home place on Thickety from Florida where he had worked since WWII. I'm looking forward to seeing him again. I phoned him a while back, and he remembered the well digging and the dynamiting. We had a good laugh.

I'm looking forward to several more years of living alone as long as I have good health and the energy to do the things that need to be done. I still enjoy living. I would not care to live on if I were beyond doing for myself and had to depend on others for all my needs. Only the Good Lord knows my future and my daily needs. I can carry on only by help and guidance from Him.

I love my children, my grandchildren, and my great-grandchildren. I pray for them and wish them the best things in life. I hope that they never forget me and that they know they will always be welcome at grandpa's house.

# SHORT STORIES

## OLD RED, THE ROOSTER

While I was growing up in the mountains of Western North Carolina, my lifestyle was no different from that of any of the other young people around me. We were all victims of the Great Depression. We were taught to work, and everyone in a family had certain things to take care of. One would do the milking; another would feed the cows and hogs. Usually, the girls would feed the chickens and gather the eggs.

Speaking of chickens reminds me of the biggest, meanest, and bravest chicken in the mountains. He was a big Rhode Island Red rooster we owned. His family consisted of eight mixed-breed hens and six capons. They were one big happy family, and everything that they did was centered on "Old Red." He protected them from the cats, the dogs, the chicken hawks, and anything that he thought would upset his family. He would even ruffle up his feathers if an airplane passed overhead.

Everything was not always rosy for Old Red. He had a few problems every now and then. One time what would have been a little problem turned out to be a big one for Old Red. It happened when all of the hens either were setting on their eggs waiting for them to hatch, or the already had a clutch of little chicks. The problem for Old Red was that the hens setting or the ones with little chicks would not let him anywhere near them. If he got to close they would flog and peck him. They had him "hen pecked." He had to keep at a safe distance.

Well, Old Red was getting mighty lonesome walking around all by himself. He needed someone to hang out with. The only thing to do was to get friendly with the capons. Now, everyone should know what a capon is. It is not a male rooster, nor is it a female hen. A capon had some minor surgery when it was a very small chick. This surgery was performed by my dad. All he used was his pocket knife to do the surgery.

The capons were going along in their happy-go-lucky way, never suspecting that they were being watched real close by Old Red. Old Red joined in with them, clucking and trying to be one of the boys. Now, these capons looked like roosters, walked like roosters, but didn't act like roosters. They liked to be left alone and didn't want to hang out with the other chickens, including Old Red.

Old Red decided he would change their way of thinking. He would let them know who ran things around the barn and the yard. He picked out the largest of the capons and started picking on him. He his plan was to get a fight going and give this capon a good whipping, and the others would be afraid to talk back to him.

Well, it wasn't as easy as Old Red had planned. The capon he chose to fight was sort of stubborn. Since this capon was the largest of the gang, he was looked upon by the others as their leader, and he was determined to keep it this way.

Old Red ruffled up his feathers and ran toward the capon. The capon saw him coming, and he braced himself for the first blow of the showdown. Old Red didn't expect the capon to put up a fight. This was not going as planned. The capon got in the next blow. He hit Old Red so hard that he ended up on his back. Up he jumped, feathers ruffled and in a hard run. He met the capon head on. They both staggered a little and began to walk around each other. All the other capons and a few of the hens that had left their nests were watching.

While watching Old Red, the capon was looking for an opening to get out of this fight before he lost any of his pretty feathers. He was near the woods. He saw his opening, and he headed to the woods. All the other capons joined him and, soon it was all over.

Old Red was really proud. He had won the battle and was still the boss around the farm. He flapped his wings, put his head up high, and let out a crow that was so loud that it scared the few hens that had been watching the fight.

From that day on, the hens and Old Red didn't keep company with the capons. This suited the capons just fine. They loved the peace and quiet of the woods.

# OLD RED AND THE WORM

One of the many places where we lived was in a house located up one of the deep hollows of Little Sam Mountain. There were no level places to build a house, so it was built on wooden poles. In this kind of mountainside house, the front was usually five or six feet high while the back was touching the ground. All the buildings were built to fit on a sloping hillside. This included the outside toilet. It was built from rough lumber. We had what you would call a deluxe model: it was a two-seater.

The outhouse was a very popular meeting place for the womenfolk to sit and gossip. The menfolk would use it for reading or simply as a resting place. Of course, it was also used for what it was built for.

We had an uncle who would visit pretty often, and the outhouse was his favorite place to relax and meditate. When asked why he stayed so long, he usually said he was reading about the latest farm equipment in the Sears Roebuck or Montgomery Ward catalogs that were always there. We used them for our toilet paper.

This was also a special building for Old Red, our Rhode Island Red Rooster. He was a very smart chicken and knew where all the good things in life were. He dearly loved worms as one of his favorite meals, and there was no better place to find them than under the outhouse. He would make a couple of trips there every day checking for worms.

Now, this uncle was visiting one day, and it just so happened that he and Old Red paid a visit to the outhouse at about the same time. Uncle was relaxed, catching up on his reading, and Old Red was checking out everything below, looking for the big fat worms. Red happened to look up. He batted his eyes, shook his head, and all at once he leaped up. Uncle let out a blood-curdling scream, and out of the outhouse he ran trying to get his overalls on. Old Red now knew that what he had thought was a giant worm was not a worm after all. He to started running in a direction opposite from the way Uncle was going.

After Uncle regained his breath, he asked, "Where do you keep the shotgun? I'm going to kill that crazy rooster."

No one was about to help him. The whole family liked Old Red. He kept the farm yard safe for all the other animals. So, Uncle cut his visit short. He packed up and went to visit some of his other relatives, and Old Red came out of hiding. We all knew that we wouldn't be seeing this uncle again any time soon.

## OLD RED AND THE NEW ROOSTER

Everything was going pretty good for Old Red, but he was getting older and had slowed down quite a bit. He no longer paid any attention to the capons, and he paid less attention to his family than before. The family had grown larger during the past year. There were all the old hens and ten new young pullets. There was also a young rooster along with several new young capons, and you could see that the young rooster was the son of Old Red. He was hatched in the early spring and had survived Dad's pocket knife surgery.

One day Old Red began to notice that there was a change taking place in his family. Nearly all the old hens and a few of the pullets began to hang out more with the young rooster. He had started crowing, but it was nothing like the sound Old Red made when he crowed. The young rooster was just getting started, and I guess you could say that his voice was changing. Anyway, this began to bother Old Red. The young rooster would start crowing between four and five o'clock every morning, the way Old Red had done when he was young. Lately, Old Red would start crowing sometime after six o'clock in the morning.

The early crowing and the way the hens and pullets were acting began to be quite a concern for Old Red. He didn't like it at all, so he began to make plans to change a few things around the farm. He wanted things to be like they were before the new young rooster came along. He simply was not getting the attention he deserved or the respect he should be getting; after all, he was the chickens' protection from the cats, the dogs, and any other critter that came their way.

Old Red thought to himself, *I know what I'll do. I'll give that smart young rooster a good whipping, and that will put him back in his place.*

This seemed to be an easy task to Old Red, but he had forgotten that he wasn't as young as he once was, and that the young rooster was a lot quicker than he was. The young rooster wasn't as big or as heavy as Old Red, but he was a pretty smart bird—after all, he was the son of Old Red.

One day the young rooster was scratching around looking for earthworms. He found one and began to cluck: "Cluck. Cluck-cluck" (chicken talk). Almost all of the hens and pullets ran to the young rooster. Old Red saw this, and the blood shot to his face. He decided right then and there to put a stop to this nonsense. He ruffled up his feathers and started toward the young rooster as fast as his legs would carry him. The young rooster saw him coming, but he didn't budge. He ruffled up his feathers and was ready to do battle with Old Red. He had a good thing going and was not about to give it up without a fight.

The young rooster glanced around and right away he new that Old Red was about to give him a good flogging. He jumped as high as he could, and Old Red scooted right under him. The first thing Old Red knew, the young rooster was sitting on his back and pecking and chewing his comb. Old Red regained his balance and was all over the young rooster. He started giving him a good flogging. The blood from his comb was running down into his eyes. This had never happened to Old Red before. Finally, the young rooster and Old Red decided to call the fight a draw. Each one began to slowly move away from the other. The old hens gathered around Old Red feeling sorry for him and clucking to tell him that they still liked him; but from that day on, it looked like the "Young Rooster" would be the big boss over our chicken flock.

## CHICKEN AND DUMPLINS

Well, things were going pretty smooth around the farm, especially with Old Red. He had decided to take an early retirement and let the young rooster handle all the daily chores. After all, he had watched over his family for more than three years. In the life of a chicken, this was a very long time.

As for the young rooster, all the hens were looking to him to supply all their daily needs and protect them from the other animals. This was a pretty big job for him because the number of hens in the flock had increased from eight to twelve. There were also the capons that the young rooster had to protect, but protection was all he gave them. He had no interest in where they went or what they did; he had all he could handle with the twelve hens. Also, the young pullets expected more attention from him than the old hens did.

Egg production had increased; more little chicks were being hatched; and my Dad started to notice the young rooster more. He began think: "Why are we keeping an old rooster when we don't need him? All he does is sit around in the shade and eat. He's getting so fat that he could have a heart attack. But, on the other hand, I don't think that any of the family, including me, could eat him if we decided to make a Sunday meal of chicken and dumplin's. I've got to come up with a plan to get rid of Old Red."

Getting rid of Old Red was not as big a problem as Dad thought it would be. He was talking to a neighbor who lived up the hollow from where we lived, and it so happened that he, too, had the same problem that we had. He had an extra rooster to get rid of, and no one in his family wanted to eat him.

"Why don't we just trade roosters," Dad said. "I'll give you Old Red for your Winedot rooster and a half bushel of corn."

"Why do you want me to give you my rooster *and* the corn?" the neighbor asked.

"Well, Old Red is a lot larger than your rooster, and he is as fat as mud. Your rooster will have to be put in a coop and fattened up before we can eat him," Dad told him.

"All right. It's a deal," the neighbor agreed. "I'll bring my rooster over tomorrow and get your old red rooster." Everything was working out pretty well with getting rid of Old Red.

It so happened that, in about three weeks, the circuit-rider preacher would be coming to hold the annual three-week revival meeting at the local Baptist Church. This preacher had to be fed and given a place to sleep during the time he would be here for the revival. Of course everyone knows that a Baptist revival preacher's favorite food is chicken. He doesn't care how you cook it as long as you have it at meal time and there is enough to have a second helping.

To get your name mentioned and be praised for what a fine meal you served before the preaching started, you had to have the preacher over to your house for a meal. The womenfolk very much liked to get this recognition. Seeing who could get their names mentioned during a revival meeting was sort of like a contest to them. They wanted to be able to brag about all the compliments they got from the preacher about their chicken, their apple cobbler, their biscuits, and all the other good food they had on the table when the preacher came to their house for dinner.

We had never had a preacher come to have dinner with us. I guess it was because my Mom didn't think that she could compete with the other women because we never had a chicken that we could spare for the preacher's dinner. But now, trading Old Red had given us our first chance to feed the preacher. Mom was all excited about it, and she began to plan a meal like we had never seen in our whole lifetime. She meant to see to it that the preacher would really brag on her cooking.

The time finally came. We were to feed the preacher on the second Sunday of the revival meeting. Things were really buzzing around the house. Everyone had to keep out of the way so Mom could get everything ready.

The preacher was ready to eat as soon as he got to our house. After he said a long prayer blessing the food, we were *all* ready to eat. The preacher got first choice of the food. Mom had cooked the most chicken and dumplin's we had ever seen. She had added extra milk and a lot of extra dumplin's to the Winedot rooster. After eating several helpings of chicken and dumplings and apple cobbler, the preacher burped real loud and said, "This is the finest meal I've ever had. I think I'll go upstairs and take a short nap before the services begin."

I guess this was the day that Mom had been looking forward to. She was really happy, and all of this was made possible by Old Red. He had supplied the chicken and dumplins for Mom's special meal.

## A ROOSTER FOR DINNER

The revival meeting was over, the preacher was gone, and there were a lot fewer chickens in the hollow than there were before the revival. This reduction in the chicken population included the departure of Old Red, too. Feeding the revival preacher also took its toll of capons. (The smart ones had hid out in the woods until everything got back to normal.) Our family enjoyed the great meals we had during the revival because we usually only ate vegetables and corn bread. Chicken on the table was for special occasions only.

Everything around the farm was back to normal. The young rooster had calmed his flock down, and they were over their nervous spell. The egg production was getting better, and the young rooster was getting cockier everyday. Sometimes he would attempt to flog and fight some of the family. He wasn't afraid of anything. He was also venturing out of his territory.

Wherever we lived in the mountains of Western North Carolina, we kept our house cool in the summer months by leaving all the windows and doors open. This would let the cool air from the mountains flow through the house. We could regulate the temperature of the house by opening or closing the windows and doors.

At this time, we were living in a house in Buckeye Cove, near Canton, North Carolina. One day, Mom had our mid-day meal on the dinning table. For some reason, she had to leave the room for a few minutes. It so happened that the young rooster was on the back porch at the time. I don't know if a rooster can smell or not, but, just the same, this one spotted the food on the table and also noticed that there was no one around. Into the house he went. With one big jump, he was on the table. Once there, he began to help himself to our dinner.

When Mom came back and saw what was taking place, she let out a yell and made a dive for that rooster. Down from the table he hopped; then he ran out the back door and to the barn as fast as he could go.

When we came in to eat lunch, Mom told us what had happened. I began to plan what to do because I figured that this was not the last time for a visit from that rooster. I got me a large "poke" (a paper bag), a hand full of dried beans, and some string. I put the dried beans into the poke and then blew air into the poke. When it was full of air, I tied it real tight. It looked sort of like a basketball. I was ready for that rooster when he "came to dinner" again.

Sure enough, a couple of days later, here he comes. Mom and I hid so he couldn't see us. Up, onto the table he went. I ran around the house and shut the door so he couldn't escape. Then I grabbed him by the legs, took him outside, and tied the bean-filled poke to one of his legs. I turned him loose, and he started running. The bean bag was following right behind him. He stopped and began to try to fight whatever it was that was following him. He made a terrible racket. Whenever he turned, so did his enemy. There was nothing he could do but to try to run away from it; but he couldn't outrun it. Soon, he was so tired that he gave up and fell over on the ground.

I figured he had learned a lesson, so I cut the string and removed the poke. After a few minutes he got his wind back and decided to run some more. Off he went, and he noticed that there wasn't anything chasing him. He stopped, flapped his wings, put his head as high as he could, and crowed the loudest he had ever crowed. He was telling everyone that he had won the fight. Be that as it may, from that day on, that rooster never came into the house for dinner again.

# MY DOG AND THE BOBCAT

When I was growing up in the 1930s, every young boy had a dog that he could call *his* dog. This was true with about all the young boys in the mountains of Western North Carolina. It had been this way for over a hundred years, but I don't think that this is the way it is now. A boy's dog and hunting trips were part of our growing up. We didn't have TV or computer games. We also walked everywhere we went. A boy having a car was unheard of. If we wanted to go somewhere, we had two choices: either to walk or to ride a horse. I usually chose to walk, especially in the summer. When it was hot, the horse would sweat a lot, and you would have to go to the creek and take a bath after riding because the smell that got on you from the horse was awful.

Back to my dog. My dog was not of any certain breed. If I were to guess, I would say that he was part bulldog (the small breed), and part feist (the Rat Terrier type). Most of all, he was *my* dog. When I was home and had all my chores done, I would take "Spot" (that was his name), and we would go into the woods to hunt. We didn't care what kind of animal we found, whether it be a ground squirrel, a field mouse, a rabbit, or anything, as long as it was small enough so that Spot could handle it. That dog did more barking and digging than he did catching. Anyway, we were hunters, and that was good enough for me and Spot.

There was a family named Lindsey who lived in the same area that we lived in, the Beaverdam Township. I guess the name of the place was chosen long ago because beavers were always damming the creek and causing water to flood the fields nearby. There were two boys in the Lindsey family who were always asking my Dad to take them hunting.

The Lindsey boys had some dogs, but they wouldn't tree a raccoon or a possum. They were rabbit dogs. Dad always kept good hunting dogs. They were always either a bluetick or a redbone breed. His dogs were not allowed to run loose except when they were on a hunting trip. These dogs were a part of our family, and we always treated them very well. My Dad and the Lindsey boys planned a hunting trip, and I was invited to go along. I was not allowed to bring my dog, Spot. He wanted to run and play a lot, and Dad's dogs were all business. Spot had to stay home.

Most of our hunting was done at night because everyone had to work during the daylight hours. We didn't have any flashlights, only lanterns for light to see our way by and to spot whatever the dogs treed. We filled some lanterns with oil. Dad got his .22 caliber gun ready, and the Lindsey boys had their sling shots and plenty of stones for ammunition. Everyone was excited and ready to get started.

We headed to the watersheds on the mountains at the head of Beaverdam Creek. There was a noise behind us. Dad raised the lantern above his head and there he saw Spot. Spot had made up his mind that he was just as good at hunting as the big dogs, and he was not going to be left out of this "big hunt." We were so far from home that everyone was willing to let my dog come along, but I had to keep him away from the hounds. I agreed to do this.

After about an hour, we were at the foot of the mountain where we were going to hunt for 'coons. We turned the hounds loose, and everyone spoke the familiar words: "Go get 'em, Ol' Blue! Go, Red! Go, boy!" Those hounds knew exactly what they were supposed to do. This was a big night for them, too. They were born to hunt, and they seemed to enjoy it very much.

We kept walking deeper into the mountain forest. Everything was very quiet. We kept going, and every little while Dad or one of the boys would yell out a loud, "Go get 'em, Blue." Soon, we heard one of the dogs begin to let out a long bark every once in a while.

"He's picked up a scent," someone said.

Soon, both dogs were barking, and they were "beginning to sing," according to Dad.

"It won't be long," one of the Lindsey boys said.

Those hounds were going at it hot and heavy. You could tell that they were getting close to their prey. The trail was real hot. We wouldn't have much longer to wait. They would have him "up a tree" soon.

We kept walking as fast as we could toward the sound of the dogs' barking. Then there came what we had been listening for, that "tree" bark. They had something up a tree. We had to hurry to give them some help getting whatever it was out of the tree and on the ground so they could have some fun fighting it.

After what seemed to be forever—climbing up rock cliffs, wading through creeks and spring drains, down on our knees crawling through the thick underbrush, getting scratched from briers—we finally got to the place where the dogs were keeping something up a big tree. Dad put the lantern on his head and began to search the tree.

"There he is. Sittin' in the top, as high as he can get," he said. "You boys see if you can knock him out with your slingshots. I don't want to shoot him unless I have to. The dogs need to have some fun first."

The Lindsey boys got their slingshots out of their overall pockets, each selected a good round rock from their front pockets, and they began to look for eyes shining up in the tree. Every time the critter in the tree looked at the light from the lantern, its eyes would shine like coals of fire.

Flip. Here went a rock. "Missed him," the youngest boy said.

Flip. Flip. More rocks up into the tree. "Got 'im," one of the boys yelled. "He's comin' down." They both had hit him.

"Hold the dogs."

"Wonder what it is?"

"Could be a 'coon."

Down it came. "Bam!" It hit the ground.

"Lord have mercy!" one of the Lindsey boys yelled. "It's a bobcat! And a big un' at that. Turn them dogs loose."

Things were really getting exciting, and the dogs were ready to get that cat. They knew from experience how to "nip" their prey and not let it get hold of them. But this wasn't the way my dog looked at it. The hounds were making more noise than they were biting that cat. Well, *my* dog had other thoughts about what was going on. *I'll show this bunch who really is the brave one around here,* he must have thought.

The hounds had the bobcat backed up against a big rock cliff. Here went Old Spot, right between the two hounds and right at that cat. The bobcat jumped up, and Spot ran right under it. The cat landed square on Spot's back, and it sunk its long, sharp claws into him. My dog was trying to get free of the cat, but the cat wouldn't let go.

Off down the mountainside went Spot with that cat riding him like a cowboy rides a horse. The last thing we heard was Spot trying to tell someone to help him get loose from that cat. The hounds had been tied up to keep them from following my dog and the bobcat.

Soon, everything was really quiet—no Spot and no bobcat. We waited for my dog to come back so we could get on with our hunting. We waited for nearly an hour, and still there was no sign of Spot.

That was nearly seventy-five years ago, and to this day I don't know what happened to Spot. Only that bobcat could tell us what really happened that night. This is a true account of what went on that night when I went hunting and my dog caught a bobcat.

# BLACKBERRY COBBLER

There are many ways to make a cobbler—with peaches, apples, pears, blueberries, and even figs—but none of these can take the place of the old standby, *blackberry* cobbler. And to enjoy it the most, you must pick the blackberries yourself.

One of the many chores that my brother, TJ, and I had during the summer months when not in school was picking blackberries. We picked them not only for our table but also for sale to the "city folks." They would pay us ten cents (10¢) a gallon for our berries.

One day in summer we were up early, long before daybreak, and we headed to the mountain where the berries were big and plentiful along the edge of the woods. On this day we were going to the mountain that our Grandpa Pressley owned. He had one side of Pressley Mountain, and the Pattons owned the other side. Although they were wealthy, they would take half of your berries if you picked any on their side of the mountain. We always traveled on our side, but sometimes we did venture onto the Patton side because their berries were never picked. By noon we had our buckets full of big juicy berries. We had about five gallons total. That meant four gallons for sale and one gallon for our favorite cobbler.

It so happened that my little white dog had come along with us to the berry fields. This was okay with us until something strange happened. Without warning, my dog began to run around in circles, barking and crying like he was going mad. This scared the living daylights out of TJ and me. We didn't know what was happening, so we both climbed up a tree where we would be safe from the dog in case he had gone mad. After running around in circles and making a lot of noise he stopped and seemed to be back to normal. We came down from the tree, got our buckets of berries, and went on our way.

We were not far from the main road. Taking it would be a lot easier walk home than climbing back up the mountain. We never gave any thought about being on the Patton side of the mountain. Soon we were down onto the road and on our way home. Suddenly two of the Patton boys appeared; where they came from we didn't know. They were near twenty years old, and we were not yet teens. They said that we had picked the berries from their mother's property and that half of the berries belonged to them. They made us go to their house and took us into the kitchen. There, a woman was working over a hot, wood-burning stove.

The boys said, "Look here. We have some berries for you to can."

"I don't have time for 'em," she said. Then she gave us permission to leave.

We were on the road again to take four gallons of berries to town to sell for forty cents. Then it happened again. My dog began another one of his fits. He was running all over the road. It was very rare to see a car pass by on this road, but one just did happen to come by. My dog ran in front of the car, and it hit him and killed him instantly. TJ let out a whoop.

Well, I had lost my little dog, but we didn't have to be afraid of the "mad dog" anymore. (Years later, I was told that these fits were caused by the dog having worms in his stomach.) Also, TJ and I had earned twenty cents each, and the whole family had a big blackberry cobbler to eat.

# CHRISTMAS, 1933

You will have to be in your 80s or close your eyes real tight to get a picture of what a Christmas was really like in the years of the Great Depression. There was no going to the store and buying the things that you would need to decorate the house or a Christmas tree. Although we were very poor, we always managed to find a way to brighten up the house and get into the happy mood for Christmas. The following is a true account of what took place at our house when the Christmas season rolled around back then. I may miss a little or add to the actual things that took place because it was a very long time in the past. After all, I am 85 years old.

We would start getting ready for Christmas in the late fall when the chinquapins started opening. I am sure that anyone under the age of 60 doesn't know anything about a chinquapin. It is a relative of the chestnut. Instead of being a tree like the chestnut, it is a shrub-like bush about five feet tall. The burrs and nuts look like those of a chestnut, but they are smaller, there is only one nut in each burr. Chinquapins were very plentiful in the 1930s in the mountains of Western North Carolina. They usually were found on the lower hillsides, not at the higher elevations like the chestnuts. They are all gone now along with the native chestnut trees. We would gather the small chinquapins and let them dry. They would become a part of our Christmas tree decorations when the time came to put up a tree for Christmas.

We could tell that it would not be long until Christmas when Mom would say, "You'd better be good because Santa Claus is watching you." My brother, TJ, and I didn't really believe in Santa, but our two sisters, who were lots younger, thought that Santa was real. Anyway, we went along with the Santa thing. We would wish for a lot of things, but we knew that we would not be getting them because there was no extra money around the house.

Also, we knew that it would not be long until Christmas when the two churches in our area would begin to get their Christmas programs together. There was the Baptist church that we attended and the Methodist church. They would plan their programs so that everyone could attend both programs. We were all neighbors, and we all shared the things that happened in our community. It would be nice if everything was the same today.

The church leaders would ask the children to do the acting in the Christmas plays. Usually it would be the young girls of the church who acted all the parts. We boys were a little shy, and, besides, the older boys would tease us if we took part in anything that included girls. The plays were put on at about the same time every year. Their theme was the birth of Christ, and that would never be changed. After all, this was, and still is, what Christmas is about. The womenfolk of the church would go all out to decorate the church. Their decorations were always pretty and original. Nothing was "store bought;" everything was handmade.

Mom began planning what we were going to have for Christmas dinner. This meal was one of very few at which we were to have some sort of meat to go along with the canned beans and the potatoes from the cellar. We would also have sweet potatoes, big biscuits ("cat heads"), thick milk gravy, and, of course, one of Mom's special stack cakes. These cakes were made with home-made cane syrup and cooked, dried apples. They were about ten or twelve layers high. If some of our neighbors killed a beef, we would have stew beef for the meat. We could get this because it cost about 10¢ a pound. If we were not having beef, we would eat a goose that we would buy from Bert Robinson. He was the janitor at the Beaverdam School. The price for a goose was somewhere from 50¢ to $1—It depended on how large the goose was.

At one week before Christmas, it was time to go get a Christmas tree. Getting a tree was TJ's and my job. We would get an axe, and off to the woods we would go. This was not a very hard job because there were plenty of pine and spruce trees to choose from. The tree had to be about five feet tall with plenty of limbs on it.

While we were out looking for the Christmas tree, the girls were busy with their job of getting the decorations ready for the tree. They strung the chinquapins using a darning needle and thread. These strings of chinquapins were garlands for hanging on the tree. The girls would make paper rings out of different colored paper that Dad had brought from the paper mill. These, too, would be put together to make a paper chain to hang on the tree.

Next came a fun part for Mom and the girls. Sometimes TJ and I would help, too. We would pop a couple of large pans of popcorn and make the popcorn into long strings. After we made the strings of popcorn, we dyed them different colors. This was done by dipping the strings of corn into different natural dyes. We used pokeberry to make a red dye. We made a brown dye from walnut hulls. We got a green dye from the bark of several types of trees.

After we had made and hung all our decorations, we would make a star from cardboard and place it in the top of the tree. Everything was now in place, and we had one of the prettiest Christmas trees in the entire community.

Next came the hanging of the stockings on the fireplace mantle. This was not an easy job because we usually didn't have any "socks." We wore our shoes without any socks. After searching through the house, we would each find a sock to put above the fireplace, even if wasn't one of our own.

The week before Christmas, we attended the Christmas programs at the two churches in our community. This was the time of the year when all the children would go to church. For a lot of them, this was the only time that they attended church for the entire year. They wouldn't miss this because after the program there was a treat for all the young children. It usually wasn't much—a couple of sticks of candy or an orange. This was a big treat for most of us because we didn't get candy or oranges very often.

On Christmas Eve everyone was excited. We would go to bed a lot earlier than usual. Santa Claus could come at any time, and if anyone was up and about in the house, he might fly on by and not stop. We would be lie really quiet in bed listening for the bells on his sleigh. We would try to stay awake as long as we could so that we might hear Santa coming to our house.

On Christmas morning we children were the first ones to get out of bed and go into the "sitting room" where the tree and our stockings were. Presents would be under the tree. Some were in brown paper bags; some were wrapped in white butcher's paper. They each had names on them.

The girls opened their gifts first. The youngest was first. Her name was on one of the white packages, and she began tearing the paper off it. Inside were a pretty new dress and some underwear. Then it was the next girl's turn. She tore off the paper wrapping on her present, and would you believe it? She also had a new dress and some underwear. I don't know if they were store bought or if Mom had made them from flour sacks. (Our flour came in cloth bags with beautiful prints on them, or you could get white ones. Nothing was wasted during those hard times.)

Next, it was time for TJ and me to open our brown paper bags. TJ was first; he had a new pair of denim pants and a blue cotton shirt. Then, I opened my bag, and I got the same things as TJ—pants and a shirt. This was great. We always got a new pair of overalls. We were getting older, and we wanted to dress differently from the little boys.

Then we went directly to the fireplace to check our stockings. Each one had the same things in it: a couple of sticks of candy, an apple, and an orange. The dresses, pants, and shirts were forgotten now.

"Don't you kids eat any of that yet!" my mother hollered. "You'll spoil your breakfast, and we have a good one this morning."

We went to the long wooden table where there were hot biscuits, fried eggs, milk gravy, apple sauce, and home-made country sausage that Mom had canned when we killed a hog last fall. This sure was great eating. We finished eating and off we went to get at that candy. Soon it was dinner-time, and we went back to the long table for another special Christmas meal.

It would be another year before this would take place again. We were all happy; no one was sick; we had enough to eat; and, most of all, we loved each other. We were thankful for what we had. During these hard times in the early 1930s, a lot of people had less than we did.

# BASEBALL IN THE 1930s

Baseball first started in the USA on the outskirts of New York City in the year 1845. It was at first an amateurs' game. The first baseball field was built in New Jersey in 1846. The first professional team was the Cincinnati Red Stockings. By the year 1867, there were more than 400 baseball teams in the USA.

In the mountains of Western North Carolina in the 1930s, information about the outside world was slow getting to us, so we didn't know anything about where and when the game of baseball began. We did know how the game was played, but we didn't always go by the rules. Usually when we were playing against another team, we agreed upon what the rules for the game were going to be before we began to play. I guess that knowledge of the game was a natural thing for nearly all young boys in the USA, sort of like the things an animal knows from the first day after birth.

I will attempt to record some of the things about the baseball experiences I had when I was growing up. I may leave out or add some things that are not as accurate as they should be. I was not the best player on our teams. My brother, TJ, was the ball player of our family. He was pretty good at any position on the team.

The most important position on the team was pitcher. Everyone wanted this spot, thinking that he was a better pitcher than anyone else. Another important position was hindcatcher. Sometimes if there was an extra player, he would be used as back-up. That is, he would be in back of the catcher in case he missed catching the ball. After the hindcatcher came all the other positions on the team. Sometimes we would have more than nine players on the field: for instance, we might have an extra outfielder and a back-up catcher.

It was pretty hard for us to get all the things that we needed for the game of baseball. The two things that were a must were a ball and a bat. It was also nice to have a ball glove or a mitt for the hindcatcher. But even a ball and a bat were hard to come by in the lean years of the 1930s. A lot of times we would play with a homemade ball and bat. We made a homemade ball by winding string, or what we would call twine, really tight until it was the size of what we thought a ball should be. Next we would apply a layer of friction tape or some melted beeswax to keep the string in place.

Our bat was often made from a piece of tree limb. It would be cut to what we though was the right length. Then it was cut and scraped to get the shape of a bat. If the wood was too green and heavy, it would be placed near the fireplace to dry out. This we called "curing."

When we played the team from Fiberville, someone on their team would have a ball, and another would have a store-bought bat. They were considered city boys. Fiberville was the village built by the paper mill for their employees, and it was within the city limits of the town of Canton, North Carolina.

The one who owned the ball usually got to play any position he wanted to; otherwise, he would take his ball and go home. However, leaving wouldn't be a wise move for him because some of the country-team boys would "convince" him that it wouldn't be the right thing to do—the game had to go on.

We liked to play the Fiberville team because they had a pretty nice field to play on. It was in the bend of the Pigeon River. The field also belonged to the paper mill, and their yard crew always kept the grass mowed and the whole area clean. When we played at home it was always in someone's cow pasture, and we had trouble finding a completely clean field. After all, this was home to the cows and horses and not a public ball field. We managed to stay away from most of the messes. Sometimes the field we played on was a little small. If there was a corn field or a pea patch nearby, you could make a lot of home runs. I guess this is where the term, "to pea patch it," came from.

We didn't always have an umpire for the game. We really didn't need one because every batter had three real strikes before he was called out. There were no called balls or strikes. With this rule the score was always very high for both teams. We usually played nine innings, but if there was time for a few extra innings before dark we would play extra innings.

In the 1930s we didn't have the luxuries of the game that the boys today have. Every town and city now has what are called "Little League" programs." All the equipment, uniforms, and coaches are furnished for these programs. These are fine programs for the boys of today. Today's boys enjoy the game the same way we did in the 1930s. Even if we had to play with limited equipment and facilities, we had lots of fun, and we were really serious about the game of baseball in the 1930s.

# THE MULE

Our neighbor owned a mule that I can never forget. This mule was not like other mules. Mules are known for their great endurance, for their strength, and for being less excitable than a horse. This was not true of Mr. Clark's mule. His mule was of the larger breed, grey or off-white in color. He was a very smart animal, but, as is the case with all mules, he was stubborn.

My dad had contracted with a widow woman to sharecrop about ten acres of land for her. He was to grow corn. She would supply all the seed and fertilizer; he would do all the work; and each would get one-half of the crop. Guess who the one was to do the plowing and planting?

Dad made arrangements with Mr. Clark to let us use his horse and mule to do our plowing and harrowing. I was told that I would be the one to do this work. I had to use two different plows—a turning plow for the bottom land and a hillside plow for the hill plowing. When plowing the bottom you never had to lift the plow. You plowed around the field until you reached the center. With the hillside plow you had to unlock the wing, lift it off the ground and swing it to the other position each time you changed directions. This was done so the dirt would always turn the same way, down the side of the hill. I could barely swing the plow to the proper position. I was about fifteen years old, skinny, and not all that stout.

To get ready, I loaded corn and corn fodder onto a wagon to feed the horse and mule their noon meals. Next, I got the collar and all the other harness on the horse and mule. I was very careful not to get behind the mule; but the horse was very gentle, and I didn't worry about being kicked by him. When I was finished with all the preparations I went off to the fields.

When I arrived where I was going, I parked the wagon in a place away from where I would be plowing. Then, I had to lead the team across a small wooden bridge over a creek. Taking the horse over was no trouble, but the mule didn't want to get on the bridge. When I finally got him to follow me, he walked across sideways, scared as could be.

Once across the bridge I hooked up and began plowing. It was soon dinner time, so I unhitched the horse and mule, took the bits from their mouths, and tied one on either side of the wagon. I then gave the mule his corn fodder. I was very careful about walking around the mule. I would talk to him so he knew where I was all the time.

Next, I took fodder to the horse, not bothering to let him know that I was behind him. He glanced back and, out of nowhere, delivered me a kick that knocked me flat on my back. To my surprise, this "gentle" horse had kicked me. I got up, brushed myself off, ate my dinner, and continued with my plowing. I didn't walk behind either the horse or the mule again without letting them know that I was there.

Mr. Clark not only did some farming, but he was also a carpenter, and he built houses for people. About this time, he was going to build a house in town for someone, and the person wanted a basement. There were no bulldozers in the 1930s to do the excavation. It had to be done with horses, a plow, and a "scoop pan." He asked me to help dig the basement. His brother-in-law, who was three years older than me, was also going to help do the job. We would use the horse and mule that I used to plow the corn field. We were to be paid $1.50 a day. This was great pay. We only got ten cents an hour for work on the farm, which would be $1.00 a day if you worked ten hours.

We loaded a wagon with a plow, a scoop pan, and feed for the team, and away we went to town and to dig the basement. You had to know four commands in order to handle a team of horses or mules. They were "gee" (go left), "haw" (go right), "gida-up" (go forward), and "whoa" (stop). This was the language that everyone used and what all horses and mules understood. Of course, you could also use the reins to pull the bits in the animals' mouths to signal them what to do: pull left, pull right, or pull back, and they would obey.

To go to the basement job we had to pass the paper mill. The paper mill used coal-fired steam engines on their trains and other moving equipment. These machines belched out black smoke and made an awful noise. The horse didn't pay any attention to them, but with the mule it was another story. He was scared to death of these things. Bill, the brother-in-law, was afraid of the mule, so it was up to me to get him around the paper mill.

That mule and I sort of knew each other, and we got along really well. He would play games with me when I tried to catch him in the lot around the barn. He would let me get close and then run to the other end of the lot. If I acted like I was giving up he would trot to the barn where I could put a bridle on him. I talked to him a lot, patted his head and nose, and when apples were in season I would give him a treat of a big red apple. He loved this.

When the mule was hitched to the wagon along with the horse, he would get scared, but the horse kept him moving in the right direction. When we quit work in the evenings we would ride the horse and mule back home. When I was going by the paper mill, that mule was always looking for one of the steam engines. It was about a half mile around the mill, and I had to ride this part of the road with him walking sideways.

My mother would pack me a lunch in a tin Soco lard bucket and would sometimes have food in a glass jar or a bowl along with a spoon or fork. I would carry the bucket back home every evening. There was a curve in the road going by the paper mill, and beyond this curve the road was straight up to the dirt road that went around the Pigeon River. I would wait until we were at the straight part of the road, and then I would get a good hold on the harness with one hand and give the bucket a good shaking. The fork and dish inside the bucket would make an awful noise. The mule would lay back his ears and take off toward home at about thirty miles an hour. I didn't hold him back, and before you could say, "Jack Robinson," I was at the Clark barn.

When I arrived at the barn, I would remove the harness from the mule and put him in his stall. Then I would feed him and leave the stall door open so he could go outside when he finished eating. While I was walking home I usually met Bill on the horse. I would do this same thing every evening while I was working on the basement.

I used that off-white mule many times after this and never had any problem with him. I knew that I could trust him to never get hurt or cause me to get hurt. We had become good friends.

# FIREPLACE COOKING

Has anyone ever told you how the family meal was prepared back when there were no gas or electric stoves?—Even back when there were no wood burning cooking stoves? All of the cooking was done over the open flames of the huge fire that was always burning in the big fireplace back then. The chimneys of these fireplaces were made of field stone and were held together with mud. They were daubed with mud so they would be airtight to make them "draw" really well and to keep sparks from the burning wood from causing a fire in the house. Most of the houses then were made from logs. There were a few made from weather-board lumber, which was never painted.

Back to the cooking. If you are not old enough to have experienced eating a meal cooked in big cast iron pots, heated by a roaring fire from burning wood logs, you have missed a meal that can not be had today. The lady of the house would do all the fixing of the food that was to go in these pots. This food usually was green beans when the garden was in and dried beans or peas in the winter months. Of course, there was always the staple food, the potato. Potatoes could be cooked several ways: boiled, mashed, and backed in the hot ashes in the fireplace. If there was meat from a recent hunting trip, there would be rabbit, squirrel, deer, or sometimes bear meat. Having meat with our meals was always a treat.

The swinging iron hooks that the pots hung on were hand-made in a blacksmith's shop. I'm not too sure how they were anchored to the stone chimney. They were probably installed between the stones when the chimney was being built.

Not only did we cook our meals in the fireplace, but we also popped corn in the evenings over the blazing fire. We had a large wire mesh corn popper with a long handle that we used for the popping. Whoever was doing the popping had to keep shaking the corn basket to keep the popcorn from burning. We would dump popper after popper of corn into a large dishpan. (This pan was the same one my mom used for washing the dirty dishes. There were no kitchen sinks or running water in our house. The closest thing we had to running water was when Mom would say, "Get the bucket, *run* to the spring, and get me a bucket of fresh *water*. This was our "running water.") When there was enough corn in the pan, Mom would melt a "print" of butter and pour it over the popped corn. Then she added a little salt. This was good eating for a bedtime snack.

Once while visiting our neighbors, the Lindsey family, I witnessed what I had never seen before and haven't seen since. One of the Lindsay household was the grandpa. He was Mrs. Lindsay's father and was considered to be an old man. He was nearing the age of sixty. Being considered old at this age was common back in the early 1900s.

Anyway, he said to his daughter, "Liz; bring me two or three eggs and some straws from the broom. I'm sort of hungry."

She brought the eggs and straws and gave them to Grandpa. He got his pocket knife from his overall pocket, carefully made a small hole in each egg and stuck a broom straw into it. He then raked out some hot ashes from the fire. Next, he placed the eggs in the ashes. He then pulled more hot ashes from the fire and put them over the eggs. Every so often he would move the straw in each egg. I guess that he was testing to see if they were cooked.

After a while, he removed the ashes, took the eggs out of the fireplace, removed the shells, and hollered, "Liz, bring me some salt."

He sprinkled the salt on the eggs and ate them. He never offered to share with me or any of the others sitting around the fire. I have never tried this method of cooking eggs, but I am sure that it would be a treat.

Many other events took place around the fireplaces in the log houses of Western North Carolina when I was growing up. Not only was the cooking simple, but all the other things that we did were simple. Things had to be this way because there was no money to purchase things from the general store. Although everything was meager and simple, you will never know how good a meal tasted from fireplace cooking.

# FUN TIME IN THE 1930s

You would think that the young people who grew up in the 1930s didn't have any fun. We didn't have any of the things that young people have today for entertainment. We didn't need these moderns things. We had lots of things to do that we enjoyed. The following are a few of the things that we did to have fun in the 1930s.

When I was young, square dances were very popular with the young folks. We didn't have telephones, but our mode of keeping everyone informed about a dance was very effective. All the boys and girls knew where the dances would be and what time they would start. The parents usually knew about the dances, too, and a lot of them wouldn't let their boys or girls go. They said that dancing was the devil's work and that it was a sin to attend such things. They were wrong. All the dances I went to had some very strict rules of behavior. If you didn't go by these rules, you would be sent home and could not come to any other dances until you decided to obey these rules. For example, you weren't allowed to bring alcoholic beverages to a dance, and fighting or profanity weren't allowed. Our dances were just some clean fun.

I went to dances at the country club in Waynesville or to the ones in the Thickety area where I lived. The ones in the Thickety area were the ones I enjoyed most. Everyone who was at these dances knew each other. People from outside the community hardly ever came to the dances in Thickety. A man who lived in the Thickety area, Arthur Ford, had made a dance hall in the loft of his barn. He installed a hardwood floor, built benches all around the walls for seating, and hung electric lights from the ceiling. Arthur, his wife, and all of his children were very good at square dancing. Arthur and his oldest son called the moves for the dances. Both were good at this.

Since we had a dance hall, all that was needed was music and dancers. This was not a problem. The boys and girls would all be there, and the band for the music was in the crowd. Nearly all the boys knew how to play some kind of stringed instrument. Who would play for a dance was decided the week before the dance took place. Sometimes there would be an older person in the band. Some of the old folks in the community also enjoyed the music and the dancing. Someone would come with a banjo, another with a fiddle, some with guitars, and another with a mandolin or a washboard. (The washboard was used instead of drums for rhythm.) Then it would be, "Let's go. Dosey doh," and away we went.

Not only did we have fun, but we got a good workout that most of us didn't need, anyhow, because we all had to do a lot of hard work around home. We had to plow, saw wood with a two-man cross-cut saw, and do other hard jobs. We put in about a ten-hour workday. It was very seldom that you would see an overweight person.

We had corn shuckings in the fall after a farmer gathered his corn from the fields. The farmer would haul his ears of corn to a spot near his corncrib and pile them in a heap that looked like a small mountain. Then word was passed around that there would be a corn shucking at a certain time and place.

The last corn shucking that I went to was one held for a farmer named Sam Robinson. It didn't attract too many older people; mostly ones who were young came to it. The corn shucking helped Sam get his corn ready to go into the crib, and it gave boys and girls a chance to get together for a night of fun. A big meal of good country cooking was always served. The host farmer had to feed the crowd at midnight. This was a job for his wife who usually recruited some help from the neighbors. A corn shucking was very common in our section of the mountains of Western North Carolina. It was all a part of what we called "neighbors helping neighbors." I do not think that this is the way it is today.

Now what do you think went on at a corn shucking? The first and most important thing was to find a girl who would sit with you at some place around the big pile of corn. The work consisted of removing the shuck (the husk) from the ears and throwing the shuck in one pile and the corn in another. If you were lucky enough to find an ear of corn that was red, you could trade it to any of the girls for a kiss. These kisses were not the long, hanging-on kind. They were only a short, peck-type of kiss. Some of the boys would secretly bring a few ears of red corn from home just in case they didn't find one. The lighting was not the same as at the square dances: Lanterns were hung around the corn pile.

We shucked corn until midnight. Then we stopped working, washed our hands, and went to the house where there would be a meal fit for a king. There was country ham, fried chicken, and sometimes stewed beef that came from "Mason" jars in which it had been canned when a beef had been killed. (Canning was the way that food was preserved because there were no freezers back then. In fact, very few homes had electrical service.) There would always be plenty of vegetables, and a favorite with everyone was the big hot biscuits with freshly churned butter. And there would also be several pies and cakes. If you wanted something to drink with your meal, you had a choice of water, coffee, or milk. We didn't have Cokes (colas) or other soft drinks.

Other things we would do to have fun were "chicken stews," "candy pullings," and the plain old party. At parties we played games like "spin the bottle" and "post office." All the games involved a girl and a boy. Spin the bottle was a simple game, as were all the others that we played. We would form a circle in the middle of the room, sitting on the floor. We would put a glass bottle on the floor in the center of the ring. Someone would be chosen to start the game by giving the bottle a spin. When the bottle stopped turning, the person it was pointing to would go to another room with the one who spun the bottle, close the door, and the two of them were alone. The girl and boy would talk or do a little hugging. If the others in the ring thought that the pair had been alone long enough, they would have someone open the door and make them come out so the game could continue. This went on until everyone had a chance to be alone with someone of the opposite gender. When spinning the bottle, if a boy was spinning and it pointed to another boy, he would spin again until it pointed to a girl. The same rule applied to a girl: she spun the bottle until it pointed to a boy. It was a simple game, but very effective. Post office was also played so that a boy and a girl got to be alone together in a separate room for a few minutes. Usually the person who was having the party would start the game by going into a room that was called "the post office." This person would start the game by asking for someone to come into the post office. That person would go into the post office, and the time the two were together there was controlled by the crowd in the same way as it was in the spin the bottle game. To "stamp" a letter meant to give a kiss to the other person who was in the post office. When time was up, the one who started the game would come out, and the one left in the room would ask for someone else to come in. This would continue until everyone had a chance to mail a letter in the post office.

 Candy pulling was one way of getting together that we all liked because we got to sample our work. Usually at a candy pulling you would know who your partner would be for the evening, and the two of you would work together. The girls always did the preparing of the candy for pulling. This was done by mixing syrup (homemade) and sugar. The ingredients would be put in a large pot and placed on the kitchen wood-burning stove. The girls knew the time that it had to be boiled so that it was just right for "pulling." Each couple would receive a portion of the mixture on a dinner plate. The couples would pull and roll it into candy. After pulling, the concoction started to get firm, and the couples would roll it into a long stick and cut it into pieces about one inch long. That was it. To hear about it, the candy pulling may not appear to have been very exciting, but it served the purpose that it was supposed to: It brought boys and girls together along with their friends. We all had a good time.

The chicken stew was not as exciting as the other things we did because it involved young married couples gathering at one of the couples' homes and exchanging the latest news, telling jokes, and singing the latest country songs. Of course, they had to have something to eat later on during the evening. The host would supply all the things needed for this "midnight supper" except the chickens. The chickens had to be supplied by the guests. First, there would be a lot of discussion about who would get the chickens, and then the job of going and getting some chickens would be given to two of the young men.

Once, my uncle Clifford (who was about 18 months older than I) and I were chosen to get the chickens for the night's stew. We went off find some chickens and started talking to each other trying to decide where we would "borrow" the chickens. Clifford said that a man and wife who lived nearby were both deaf and dumb. They had lots of chickens, and their hen house was pretty far from their house. This information brought us to a decision: They would furnish the chickens for our stew. After all, if the chickens started making a noise they wouldn't hear them.

Clifford went into the chicken house and handed me a nice fat hen. He then came out with another for himself. We went back to the house where the stew was being held, and someone dressed and cut up the chickens into small pieces. These pieces were then placed in a big pot on the kitchen stove, and the girls took it from there. The women cooked the chickens a while and then added flour and milk to make a thick cream gravy. They also made a batch of biscuits to be eaten with the stew. When everything was ready, we all each had a good helping of the stew. Everyone went home happy. Mr. King wouldn't miss the two chickens, and we would replace them someday if we ever had some chickens of our own.

I often wish that my children and grandchildren could enjoy the things that we did. It was good clean fun and cost very little. We called it fun.

# MY ENGLISH VACATION, 1944

It was 1943, and I was stationed at Fort Dix near Trenton, New Jersey. I knew that I would be moving soon, but I didn't know where I'd be going. In December of 1943 we were told that we were moving and what to pack. The next thing we did was to board a train in Trenton. We soon arrived in New York City. We marched to the docks and boarded a large ship. It was a French ship called the *Ile de France*. After we were onboard, the ship started moving down the river toward the open sea. After two days, the ship turned around and went back to the docks in New York. We were told that there had been a fire on the ship and that we would be getting off. I was glad because at every meal we were served cabbage. I thought that the French must have loved cabbage.

We left the ship on Christmas Eve, and as we marched to the train station the last-minute shoppers began cheering for us and giving us bottles of wine and whiskey. They thought that we were returning from the war front in Africa. We didn't dare spoil a good thing by telling them differently. We did look pretty bad. No one had shaved or taken a bath for over two days on the ship.

We boarded a train and went to some Army camp. I have never learned what camp it was or where it was located. We were not allowed to make any telephone calls or have any contact with anyone outside the camp. Our stay was short, and we were back on a train about two days later. We went back to the docks in New York. We boarded a much larger ship this time. Also, it was extra clean and very attractive. All the furnishings had been removed and canvas hammocks had been installed. We learned that this ship was the

*Queen Elizabeth*. We were told that there were 15,000 troops aboard and that we would be crossing the Atlantic Ocean without an escort. We were going to sail via the Arctic region where submarines couldn't go because of all the ice in the water. Our course took us close to Iceland.

I was on this ship for more than six days. On the last day onboard, we saw a lot of blimps in the air. We learned that they were watching for subs that might try to get at the *Queen Elizabeth*. We were in the Firth of Clyde off the coast of Scotland. The ship was so large that it couldn't dock, and we were taken ashore by smaller boats.

Then we got back on a train again. These trains were not like the ones in the US. They had compartments that would seat about eight people. I think there were ten or twelve soldiers in the compartment I was in. We were heading south. The first stop was near a town by the name of Chester. We were given bunks in buildings that looked like big steel pipes cut in half. These buildings were called "Nissen Huts." Our bunks had a long sack of straw on them. These mattresses were called "pallisters." Sleeping on a straw tick was nothing new for me. We often used them back in the mountains of Western North Carolina.

Chester had a wall went all the way around the town. I had never seen a town with a high stone wall around it before. There were lower and upper walkways around the inside of the wall. We didn't stay at this town but a few weeks, but I have something to remember Chester by: I have a tattoo on my arm that I got there.

Soon we were back on the train again going south to a destination unknown to us. These moves not only confused the Germans; they kept all of us guessing. When we stopped and got off the train this time we were in a place that had what looked like small mountains. This place was called Malvern Hills. We marched to what was called Blackmore Park. Here again, our living quarters and beds were like the ones we had in Chester. I learned later that there were several other Army camps in this area during the War.

There were a lot of farms around there, and most of them were using Italian prisoners of war (POWs) to help do farm work. They had been captured and sent to prison camps in England. There were no guards watching them, and you wouldn't know that they were prisoners if you hadn't seen the big letters, "P-O-W," printed on the backs of their shirts. Although we resented their getting the attention of the pretty English girls, they filled a great need for help on the farms because all the able-bodied English men were in the British military. They not only helped the farmers, but they were also working for their room and board. They were not allowed to go to the pubs or to any other public places. Their home away from home was on the farm. I don't think that there were any complaints from them. This was far better than being in a prison camp.

One day I had a 24-hour pass, and I had plans to go to Worcester. Worcester was a very nice town that was not too far from Malvern. I checked out a bike and headed toward Worcester. I passed a building that I had never noticed before. Being the curious person that I am, I decided to investigate it. Once inside I saw that it was not an ordinary place. I saw two people working over a dead body. I realized that I was in a morgue and that these people were doing an autopsy on someone. I began to ask questions. There was another dead body on another table close by. I saw that both of these dead people were black. I asked who they were, and one of the workers explained that they were two American soldiers who had shot each other, and they were determining how they had died. I asked to watch, and they said it was okay with them if I thought I wanted to. I watched while they cut and removed different parts of the bodies and weighed everything that they removed. Soon I had seen enough. I could see what had killed them. One had been shot in the head, and the other had been shot in the chest. I was told that they had shot each other while fighting.

There was a pub near Worcester that I liked to stop at. I enjoyed joining in with the local people, and I made many friends this way. The people in the pub always had a bit of news about the War. Of course, they always had dart games going on, and I was invited to join them, and I did. They were good at darts, but I was lucky even to hit the board, and I never hit the center. This didn't make any difference; I was enjoying my "Limey" friends, and I think they liked me joining in. Most of the people at the pub were old, and about all of them were doing something toward helping with the war effort. Some were air raid wardens, some were plane spotters, and some were morale boosters. Several smoked pipes, and I would usually bring along a couple of tins of Prince Albert pipe tobacco that I could get at the PX. This cost me very little, and they were glad to get it. Tobacco was hard to come by in the local stores, and if any could be had, it was expensive. All the local people who I came in contact with while in England were very nice to me. I enjoyed their company very much, especially that of the girls.

While at Malvern, I made a visit to London. This was quite an experience for a country boy out of the mountains of Western North Carolina. A buddy and I boarded a train in Worcester and went to the "big city." At this time the Germans were sending a lot of what we called "buzz bombs." They were hitting London pretty heavily. All you could do when they started dropping was to find some sort of protection and hope that the bombing would pass over and not hit near you. The sirens sounded very often. I was amazed to see the people in London just stopping long enough to see where the bombs would fall and then going about their work as if nothing had happened. They sure had faith that the war would be won by the British and their allies.

I visited the famous waxworks in London. This was something to see. The dummies made from wax looked so real that I found myself talking to a doorman made of wax. I asked him for directions. Did I ever feel silly! This didn't happen again while I was there. I never told anyone about my talking to a wax dummy.

Most of my time in England was spent in the Malvern-Worcester area. I saw and heard of things that I had never known about. Some of these were "tea time," "fish and chips," "darts," and the many different kinds of beer and ale. I liked all of these new things. It didn't bother me when the ink from the newspaper that the fish and chips were wrapped in got on the fish. It still tasted good.

One of the duties of my job in the Supply unit was going along with the laundry detail to the Court Steam Laundry in Birmingham. This detail took two six-by-six truck loads of dirty laundry to the Court Steam Laundry the first of each week and returned the last of each week to pick up clean laundry. I looked forward to these trips. My job was to do the paperwork connected with having the laundry done.

The place that did our laundry employed about 100 people, and I would guess that 75 of these were women. There were all kinds of women working there. Some were skinny, some fat, some tall, some old, some young—you name it. From this wide selection, a man could find some woman that he liked. I dated two women from the Laundry. One came to Worcester on the weekends, and she and her family had me visit them on Sundays to have lunch with them. The other girl was only 17 years old. (I was 21 at the time.) She would come to Worcester on the train, and I would meet her at the station.

Whenever I met the girl at the station, I had the cooks in the mess hall make me a picnic box, and she and I would go down to the river bank and have lunch. I had to be very careful not to get caught with this girl by the one who was having me to her home for Sunday lunch. But I didn't have to slip around very long because we were getting ready to move again. Neither I nor any of the other soldiers looked forward to these moves because we knew some day soon we would be on our way to France and there be face to face with the German Army.

Once again, we were on the move going to some place we hadn't been before. Soon we were in Wales in the town of Llandudno. There we were billeted in several hotels and other buildings. Why we went there, I will never know. It was a vacation spot for the English. Those who came on vacation at this time were only allowed to spend one week there. The demand for a vacation here was great. I would guess that 95% of those who came on vacation here were women. This was great for us; we could have a different girl every seven days.

I learned the game of golf here. Some of the fellows who had played before had me join them. We played for the stakes of "two and six" for each hole. It wasn't long before all of my two and six were gone. That was okay by me. I had rather have been with the girls than playing this game.

While in Llandudno I had a strange thing happen to me when I was dating a girl from Liverpool. Instead of my giving her a sad story about the hard times in my life, she told one to me that would bring tears to your eyes. Her story was about how bad her parents treated her, how poor she was, and how she never had the things that she wanted. She asked me to write her a letter sometime. I promised to write to her. She gave me her address in Liverpool, and a few days later she was gone. I soon found out why we were here in Wales. We were "downsizing." That is, we were going to turn in all our equipment except the very minimum of things that we had to have. We all turned in our gas masks. There were two truck loads of them. They were going to be put in a warehouse in Liverpool. I was assigned to go along to do the paperwork. We found the warehouse in Liverpool, and, after one of the trucks was unloaded, I asked the driver to take me to the address of the poor girl that I had met in Wales.

He found her address easily enough. It wasn't the "cottage" that she had said it was. The house at the address she gave me was a very large stone house with a fence around it, a big iron gate, and a long walkway from the street to the front door. I looked at the address and then the house. Was I at the wrong place? I opened the gate, went to the front door, and banged the big lion's head door knocker. A lady opened the door and asked me what I wanted. I told her I was looking for a young lady by the name of Molly Dillon (not her real name).

"No one lives here by that name," she said.

About then, Molly came out and said, "It's okay, Mother. You can go now."

She asked me come into a large sitting room. I was still dumbfounded and couldn't say anything. She welcomed me to her home. I asked her why she gave me such a sad story that day we were together in Wales.

She began to explain. "I am married. My husband is in the British Army. I haven't seen him for two years. This is my mother's house, and I am staying with her until my husband returns."

We talked for a while, and I said good bye. I told her I would keep in touch.

Soon, we were on the train again, and we all knew that these moves wouldn't keep taking us to another nice place in England. As we passed through London, I knew that the only thing that would take us this far south was that we were going to a seaport. The train stopped, and several trucks were parked nearby. We left the train and got in the back of the trucks. Not long after that we passed through a gate with guards into what looked like a prison camp. It had a high wire fence all around it. We were assigned to squad tents and told that we were not to go outside the fenced area and we were not to contact anyone on the outside.

I soon found the Supply tent where I knew they would have some hot coffee. I was wrong: this Supply had tea. I found out that this staging area was run by the British Army. I noticed an English soldier who seemed really happy. He was moving around, packing a duffel bag, and humming some English song.

I said to him, "You seem awful happy."

He replied, "I am. I'm going home on furlough, and I haven't been home for about two years."

"Where are you from?" I asked.

"My home is in Liverpool," he said.

"I know a real pretty girl in Liverpool," I said. "I sure would like to see her again."

"Write her a few lines, and I will get your message to her if you know where she lives," he said. "I'll do that," I said.

The soldier left the tent for a few minutes. I asked the Supply Officer, "What's that soldier's name?"

"His name is Dillon," he told me.

A cold chill came over me. It didn't take me long to see what I was about to get into. This soldier was about six feet tall and weighed about

190 to 200 pounds. I hade a feeling that I was close to getting a good beating from the husband of the pretty girl in Liverpool. I left the Supply tent as fast as I could, and I didn't go back there again.

This was it. We were told to pack all of our belongings and be ready to ship out at 12 midnight. We were told our next stop would be Utah Beach in France. I knew right away that my "vacation" in England was over. I was leaving all of my good English friends and the good times behind, but I made a promise to myself to return someday.

## MY BIRTHDAY, 1944

It was Friday, March 31st, 1944. The next day would be my 22nd Birthday. "Sergeant," I asked, "could I have a two-day pass? My birthday is this Saturday, and I want to go to Worcester and spend the night and do a little celebrating. I'll be back Sunday evening."

"Sure," he said. "Come by tomorrow morning, and it'll be ready."

"I need a buddy to go with me. Would you give Private James Foster a pass, also? He said that he would go with me if he could get a pass."

"Okay," said the sergeant. "It's best that you always have a buddy with you when you go to town."

Off I went to tell James the good news.

Early the next morning we picked up our passes, signed out, and went on our way to Worcester and a big birthday party. James, I, and a good pub—that was all we needed for our party. We decided to walk instead of taking the bicycles that we could check out. We might forget where we left them. If we didn't check them back in, we would have to pay for them. James was a tall, lanky boy who was also from North Carolina, and, like me, he didn't mind walking to town. We were used to walking. Being in the Army, we walked everywhere we went.

We were soon at one of my favorite pubs close to Worcester. It was located on the left side of the road going into town. It was sort of like a small hotel. It was a two-story building. The pub was downstairs, and I don't know what was on the second floor. Here was where we started celebrating my birthday.

We left the pub at about four o'clock that evening and went to a hotel in Worcester that was operated by the American Red Cross. We signed in and said that we would be staying there tonight. Then we went off looking for another pub. We soon found one we liked and progressed from drinking a few beers to having a few scotches and a few gins.

I remembered that I was supposed to meet the cute, red-headed girl who worked at the Court Steam Laundry in Birmingham. She and her family were going to spend the weekend in Worcester, and I was invited to have lunch at her house and meet the other members of her family. We had plans to go to a movie at a theater down the street from the hotel this evening.

Time went by really fast, and Foster and I had many drinks before asking someone what time was it. We learned that it was by now a little after seven. I told him that I had to meet a girl at seven at the movie theater. We got up from the table, and the scotch and gin hit the bottoms of our stomachs. We had rubber legs. We managed to make it outside and start on our way to the movie house. However, we took a wrong turn and were going in the wrong direction. James was staggering and talking really loudly when two MPs came by. They got him by the arm and took him away. I found out later that they took him to the hotel and put him to bed.

As for me, I wasn't as bad off as James, but I still was not thinking straight. I went on looking for the girl that I was to meet. About then someone took my arm and said, "Where have you been? You were supposed to meet me an hour ago." We went on to the movie house with her holding my arm. She somehow managed to get me to the balcony, and there I went to sleep. Later, when she awakened me; everyone else had already gone. We left the theater, and she guided me to the hotel, where I went to bed. At about eight the next morning, someone woke me up and said that there was someone to see me downstairs. I dressed and went down to the front door. It was my girlfriend from Birmingham.

"Charles," she said. "We are expecting you at our house. You are to meet my mother, my dad, and my sister."

I asked her to give me a few minutes to wash up and dress. She told me to hurry up. A few minutes later, I was on the street in front of the hotel where she was waiting for me.

"I can't find my hat," I told her.

"Come with me," she said.

She took me to the movie house. Someone was there cleaning, and we asked if we could look around. We went to the balcony and to the seats that we were in last night, and there was my hat.

I said to Pat, "I need a drink. My head is going 'thump, thump, thump,' and I don't want to meet your family feeling like this."

She led me to a basement door around the corner. She knocked on the door; a man opened it and asked what we wanted. I didn't hear what she told him, but he invited us in. After a couple of Scotches we were on our way to meet the family and have lunch.

They were a nice family, and they welcomed me with open arms into their home. This kind of hospitality was typical of all the English people I came in contact with while in England. After lunch, Pat's father, Mr. Mottram, and I went up stairs to his study. He asked me many questions about different things back home in the USA. He wanted to know if I played golf and if I would be interested on starting a business with him in the US after the war. I told him my main concern at the moment was getting back to the US alive.

After the dishes were washed and put away, Pat knocked on the door and asked me if I was ready for a walk. I said that I would like that. I was really happy to get away from all the questions I was being asked. My head was not feeling too good yet. We walked down by the river and talked. She told me that she thought her mother and father liked me as much as she did. Soon our walk was over, and we returned to her house.

I said good bye to Pat and went back to the hotel to look for James. One of the ladies at the desk said he had signed out and gone back to the Army base. I checked out of the hotel and went back to Malvern hoping to get a good night's sleep. My birthday had passed.

This was not the last time I saw Pat. We had several dates after the one on my birthday. I began to sense that things were getting serious between her and me. I had never thought of our relationship as anything more than company and a good time. I had to break up this friendship.

On the next date we walked down by the river, and I told her a lie. I said, "Pat, we have got to stop dating each other."

"Why?" she said.

"Because I am married and have a wife in North Carolina waiting for me to come home."

She dropped her head for a moment and then looked at me and said, "That's okay. We can still have fun while you are in England."

I didn't answer. We returned to the house, and I said good bye and left.

I didn't intend to see her again. I had decided that I would find another girl for company. But she wasn't about to give up so easily. On the next weekend I stayed in camp to avoid meeting her. About noon, one of the gate guards came to my hut and said that there was someone to see me at the gate. I asked what the person looked like. He said that it was a very pretty woman with red hair. I knew who this was. I told him to tell her that I was on duty for the whole weekend. This was the last time that I heard from Pat. I did find another girl, and she was from Birmingham, also.

# THE PICNIC

It was a dark and stormy night. The rain was falling, and thunder and lightning were everywhere. Wait. This is a story with a happy ending, and it should not begin like most other stories do, so here we go.

My story starts in Worcester, England, in the year 1944. I was in the US Army and stationed in Malvern, which is near Worcester. The other character in my story is a pretty young English girl, Brenda, whom I met at the Court Steam Laundry in Birmingham. She was working in the office where I would visit twice each week to take care of business for my outfit's laundry. We had never dated because it wasn't easy for me to go to Birmingham where she lived. On one of my visits to the laundry, I invited her to come to Worcester on a Sunday morning so we could spend some time together. She planned to come to Worcester on an early train, and I would meet her at the station.

I made arrangements with the cook in the mess hall to make me a picnic lunch for two. He made sandwiches from several cold cuts and cheese. He packed them in a paper bag for easy carrying. I had a pass to go to town, and I woke up early on the Sunday morning of our date. I checked out a bicycle and went to the station to meet "my girl" from Birmingham.

The train was on time, and Brenda got off the train and started looking for me. After we exchanged warm greetings, we were off to find a good place for our picnic. Neither of us knew much about the town, so we went searching for a spot to have the picnic. We came to a river near the edge of town where there was nice grass along the banks. We decided that this was where we would have the picnic. Any place would have been fine with me as long as I was with this girl. We talked about many things. We talked about where I lived, what I liked to do, and my future plans. I didn't want Brenda to get serious about our relationship, so I told her that I was married and had a little child. Of course, this was not true. I showed her a picture of the woman that I later married, taken with her sister's little girl. Brenda was sort of disappointed but only for a little while. This didn't stop us from being friends. I also told her if things didn't go well when, and if I returned from the war, I would come back to see her.

We had a very nice picnic. I went back to the train station with her to see her off to Birmingham. After saying good bye to each other, we parted. I saw her several times after our picnic, but we couldn't schedule another get-together before I left for France. I didn't write to her for many months because I couldn't send any letters. I was always on the move in the war. I was in the 3rd Army, (General Patton's command) and didn't stay long at any place. We were always moving toward Berlin.

I did make it through the war. When it was all over and I was getting ready to go back to the USA, I asked to be sent back through England, but I was told that this wasn't possible. I had to go on back to the USA with the others on a ship. After arriving back home, I wrote a letter to Brenda addressed to her home in England. I never did receive an answer to my letter.

After I returned to North Carolina, I began to see a girl whom I had known all throughout my school years, and we made plans to be married. I told her about the girl in England and told her the girl's name. If we had a baby girl, we were going to name her "Brenda." The years went by fast, and we had two boys but never a girl. I tried again to locate Brenda. My wife and I were going to visit her if we could locate her, but we never did.

We had been married for 60 years when Marie passed away in 2004. I chose to live alone in the house that we had lived in for the past 40 years. Three years have passed, and I am making out fine doing my own housework. In December 2006 I decided to try once more to locate Brenda in England. I posted the following message in the "Where Are They Now?" section of one of Birmingham's newspapers:

My name is Charles Fletcher. I live in Cleveland Tennessee, USA. While stationed in England in 1944, I met a girl in Birmingham. She worked at the Court Steam Laundry in Smallheath. I would like to contact her or any of her family. My address is 2310 Harris Circle NW, Cleveland, Tennessee 37311.

Two weeks later I received an e-mail from Brenda's grandson, Scott Banks. The e-mail said that Brenda was alive and well, that she read my notice in the newspaper, and that she asked her grandson to contact me. It said that she is married and her last name is now Ingram. The e-mail message went on to say that any contact or letters could be posted to Brenda's address and that Brenda would like to talk with me.

I sent an e-mail reply to Scott and told him to set a date for a telephone call, and I would call. A date and time were set, and I made the call. I talked with Brenda and also with Scott and his mother, Pauline, Brenda's daughter. Since the call we have exchanged letters and pictures of our families. It is nice to have found a good friend 63 years after our picnic.

# UNCLE BOB

We were living in a section of west Canton that was called Mingus Cove. This was on the west side of a mountain called Pressley Mountain. The mountain separated the main road into town, US Route 19, from Stamey Cove. There were log houses all over the east side of this mountain. Several of my mother's aunts and uncles lived on this mountain. The one who was my favorite was Uncle Bob Putnam. He was my Grandma Pressley's brother. She had other brothers and sisters living on the mountain, but Uncle Bob was the one who I remember most.

The people who lived on the mountain didn't come off very often, only when it was necessary—that is, except for Uncle Bob. He did some farming and worked at odd jobs in Canton for the stores that were in town. One of his jobs was with the Parks-Belk department store. This was the largest clothing store in town. He was not a big, fat man, but he was always the Santa Claus at Parks-Belk for about four weeks when the Christmas season came around.

He also was appointed fire warden and game warden. I don't know if either of these jobs had any pay attached to it, but Uncle Bob did a mighty lot of bragging about his titles and his authority. He also was the one person on the mountain who the others looked up to for legal advice. In other words, he was the leader of the Putnam and Pressley clans.

Uncle Bob went to town pretty often, and on the way he would pass our house. He would usually drop in on his way to town, and it was always near dinner (lunch) time. It seemed that everyone had to eat three meals a day along with a snack before going to bed. It didn't make any difference if they didn't have a watch or clock. They always knew when it was time to eat. Uncle Bob knew that our mother would invite him to dinner. I never heard him refuse to eat with us. Dropping by for dinner also gave him a chance to tell us all the news back on the mountain. Most of the news was about whom he caught hunting out of season and who had burned a tobacco bed without asking him before burning. He usually told these people what the laws were, but, as far as I know, he never gave anyone a fine or have anyone put in jail. He only reminded them he was the law on this mountain.

After finishing eating and letting us know what he had done since the last visit, he would continue his trip to town to visit all his old friends who would always be sitting on park benches trading pocket knives, chewing tobacco, and vying with each other to see which one could tell the biggest tale. For Uncle Bob, this was really living in the fast lane. The simple things made the old folks in the mountains of Western North Carolina happy.

One summer morning, Uncle Bob stopped at our house for his visit and dinner. "Ellen," he said (Ellen was my mother's name), "school is out, and these boys don't have anything to do around here. Why don't you let me take them home with me on my way back this evening?" He was referring to TJ, my brother, and me. "They can help me hoe my corn patch, and I'll take them to the Pigeon River fishing one day."

This seemed like a really exciting invitation to TJ and me. "Mom," we begged, "please let us go. We'll mind everything Uncle Bob tells us."

"All right," Mom said. "But you can only stay one week."

"It's all settled, then," said Uncle Bob. "I'll stop by on my way back from town this evening and take them to my house."

Little did Uncle Bob know what he was getting himself into.

It was about four P.M. that evening when Uncle Bob came back to our house. "You boys ready to climb the mountain?" he asked. "We'd better get going. It'll be dark pretty soon, and the wild animals'll be out on the mountain, and I didn't bring my gun."

Things were getting exciting already, and we were not even on our way yet. There were wild animals on the mountain, all right, but Uncle Bob was teasing T J and me about the danger.

We left for Uncle Bob's house and a full week of fun. We walked on the Mingus Cove Road for a ways and then took the foot trail that led to the top of the mountain. It was narrow and rocky, and the farther we went, the steeper it became. This didn't bother uncle Bob because he had made this trip many times and was used to it. TJ and I were not used to such a steep climb; we had been on trails in the mountains a lot, but never on one this steep. Soon we were on the ridge at the top, and the going was easy.

It was nearly dark when we arrived at Uncle Bob's two-room log house. Aunt Roxie, Uncle Bob's wife, was outside in the yard waiting for uncle Bob. She was not expecting any company, and at first she didn't know us. She hadn't seen TJ and me but about twice before. She didn't go anywhere other than to visit the others who lived on the mountain. She seemed happy to have us visit after Uncle Bob told her who we were. We went inside, and Aunt Roxie got a match and lit the coal oil lamp that was on a shelf in the sitting room. This room was also the cooking and eating room. The other room was only used for sleeping. I never have figured out how they raised seven or eight children in such a small place. All of Aunt Roxie and Uncle Bob's children were grown and had left home by this time. All of them had left the mountain and settled in or near the town of Canton.

It was soon pitch dark and really quiet outside. Every once in a while you could hear an owl, "Who...who," and a couple of times we heard the blood-curdling cry of a bobcat. We didn't dare go outside even though Uncle Bob said it was safe.

"Time to hit the sack," said Uncle Bob, and he went off to the straw tick that was in the corner of the sleeping room. TJ and I were tired from climbing the mountain, and we were sound asleep really soon. Tomorrow wasn't far away with all its promise of the excitement of living in what we called "wild country."

It seemed that we had only been in bed for a short time when we heard Uncle Bob yell, "All right, boys. Time to get up. Soon be too hot to work in the corn patch."

Up we jumped. We didn't have to dress because we hadn't undressed when we went to bed. We went across the "dog trot" to the cooking-eating-sitting room. Here we saw a big country breakfast that Aunt Roxie had prepared for us.

"You work hands better eat a lot. Long time 'til dinner," said Uncle Bob. He seemed anxious to get to the field and start working on his corn.

We set out toward the field with hoes in our hands.

"Lots of weeds to chop," said Uncle Bob. "Got to get done before it gets too hot to work."

Of course, it never got really hot in the mountains. There was always a cool breeze. It was pretty well known that these mountain men never over-worked themselves. They needed a good rest before dinner and a short nap after dinner. There was nothing that was so important that it could not be put off until later.

There were about as many tree stumps as there were weeds in that corn patch. We chopped weeds for about two hours, and Uncle Bob said, "We'll take a break now and come back this evening when it gets cooler."

We quit work and headed to the house for our rest before dinner. This was fine with TJ and me. Then, after a good dinner (lunch) and another two-hour rest, we went back to the corn patch to finish chopping the weeds. If we finished the job, we were going fishing the next day, so we also had to dig some worms to use as fish bait. We were pretty busy for the rest of that day. We finished weeding the corn and had a big jar of worms. We were all set for the fishing trip.

We got up at daylight the next day, ate a good breakfast, and went outside to help get the cane fishing poles ready. Aunt Roxie was busy packing a lunch. She was going fishing with us. This was as big a treat for her as it was for TJ and me. She didn't get to go anywhere very often. About the only times she left home was when she went to visit the others who lived on the next ridge or down in the hollow.

When we were all set, off we went down the mountain toward the Stamey Cove Road and on to the fishing hole in the Pigeon River.

"How much farther is it?" we asked.

"Oh…not very far," Uncle Bob said. "We'll be there soon. Another thirty minutes, I guess."

"Do we need a fishing license?" I asked.

"No," said Uncle Bob. "I'm the game warden, and children under twelve don't need one. There won't be any problem. I'm the law."

When we got to the river, we began putting worms on our hooks. Soon, we were all fishing. Aunt Roxie caught the first one: a Horney Head about seven or eight inches long.

"Ain't that a beauty?" she said. And into the sack it went. "Gotta get a mess for supper," she said.

It wasn't long until we all had caught a fish. None of them were alike. We had Red Horse, Hog Sucker, Horney Head, and Silversides. We soon had about twenty in the "tow sack" (burlap bag).

"I guess we have enough for supper," said Uncle Bob. "We'd better head out home. I gotta scale and gut 'em so Roxie can get 'em on the fire. Better make a new cake of cornbread, too."

We gathered up and headed back toward the mountain and a good meal of fresh fish and corn bread along with a cool glass of fresh churned butter milk. After all this, we were ready for bed and dreams of what we would do tomorrow.

The next morning we were up bright and early as usual. After breakfast Uncle Bob informed us that he would be gone for most of the day. He had "some business" to take care of. He never said what kind of business it was, and we didn't ask him. It must have been something to do with his warden's job.

We loafed around doing some exploring and looking for something to do. Two young boys were not going to sit down and do nothing. Aunt Roxie made a cool drink for us that she called "beer." I don't know what she made it from, but it was very good—nice and cool and sweet. This didn't keep us from becoming bored. We had to find something to do.

Uncle Bob kept a couple of dogs, about ten cats, a cow, some chickens, and a jenny. This jenny would bray with her "hee-haw" so loud that all the people on the mountain could hear her. She, too, didn't work very hard. She only worked when the plowing had to be done or when she was needed to pull a sled to haul corn to the corn mill for grinding. Seems as if everyone and everything took life easy on this mountain.

It wasn't long until we came up with a plan that was sure to create some excitement. The cats were very friendly, and we decided to have some fun with two tom cats that were about half grown. We found some cotton string, and I held the cats in my lap. TJ took their tails and tied them together. There was a wire tied between two trees that Aunt Roxie dried clothes on when she washed. We took the cats that were tied together and put one on each side of the clothes-line wire and let them go. Each cat thought that the other was pulling its tail, so they began to squall and scratch each other. Cat hair was flying everywhere. They made an awful noise. Aunt Roxie came running to get her cats apart and to stop them from killing each other. TJ and I went looking for a hiding place. We laid low for the next few hours.

Uncle Bob came back from his business trip, and Aunt Roxie met him and told what we had done.

"You take them boys back home this minute," she said. "No waiting for tomorrow."

Uncle Bob didn't argue. He knew that she was serious.

We didn't have to do any packing because we didn't bring anything with us. Off we went down the mountain toward Mingus Cove and home. This had been a short week. There wasn't as much talking on the way back home as there had been three days earlier. We were soon home, and we didn't stick around to hear what Uncle Bob was telling our mother. We would probably hear from her later. Uncle Bob left for the mountains and his home.

*OUT WEST AND BACK*

We were never invited to visit our aunt and uncle again. After I returned from overseas after WWII, I went to visit Uncle Bob. This was in 1946. His children had built him a house on the upper end of the Stamey Cove Road and moved him off the mountain. He had an oil heating furnace and a few other things to make living easier for him and Aunt Roxie. He had quit the fire and game warden jobs but was still working as Santa Claus for the clothing store. He didn't mention the cat fight, and neither did I.

# AUTHOR'S NOTES

When writing this book about the memories of my life, I didn't go into some of the details about the things that happened to me. I only mentioned the events that took place to give the readers of this story a general picture of my eighty-five years of life. In the following notes I will add a few of the things that I didn't mention before.

OUT WEST AND BACK. There isn't much to add to this chapter except that the event that started our trip was the burning of our house. What caused the fire was never known. House fires happened often in the villages that the cotton mills built for their employees.

THE NEW SCHOOL. People who experienced the old one-room and two-room school houses of the early years of this country know the hardships that they went through to get an education. Many families didn't much encourage their children to be interested in school. These families only looked at how much work the children could do on the farm. Only the wealthy went to the better schools. Beaverdam School was a blessing, and all the children who attended this school were proud to let everyone know that they were going to the new school and getting a good education like the city people were getting.

A lot of the things that went on at Beaverdam were normal for most large schools. We had our pushing and shoving fights. No one was ever hurt very much in them. Maybe someone occasionally got a black eye or a bloody nose, which was as good as new the next day. There was a lot of discipline at our school, and our principal, Mr. Barbee, made sure that we went by the rules. It had to be this way because we had a pretty rough bunch of kids out of the hollows and mountains of western North Carolina.

I suppose that all schools down through the ages had what we called cowards and bullies. This was also a problem at the new Beaverdam School. I will relate what took place, and you can decide who the coward was and who the bully was.

There were two brothers at this school who had the idea that they were better than any of the other students because their parents were what we called "wealthy." They weren't really wealthy; their parents just had a big house and a little money saved that they hadn't lost during the Great Depression. They were always pushing the smaller boys around. It so happened that I was one of these boys who they tried to push around. I held my own with the brother who was my size, but I was afraid of the other one who was about twice my size.

Several boys would take a round-about route when going to town to keep from passing the bullies' house because if they caught you alone, the two would jump you. They lived on the most direct route to town, so we took a different route, although it was at least a half a mile farther this way. This soon came to an end, however.

It was the last day of the school year, and we were starting our summer break. These brothers decided to give me a good going over on this last day of school. They hurried to the cut-bank in the road leading to the area where our house was at the time, and they grabbed me and threw me on the ground. The larger boy was holding me, and the smaller one was just pushing me around. They weren't hurting me; they just wanted to make the others who were watching thought they were tough.

It happened that my brother, T.J., had stayed behind at school to bat a few baseballs. He had always loved baseball. He had a ball bat with him that we had made from a small tree. We had removed the bark and shaped it to look like a real, store-bought bat. We had to play the game without any equipment. The only player who used a glove was the catcher, and we all were too poor to own anything that you had to buy. Well, T.J. came upon the roughing up that I was getting from these boys.

The big boy was over me holding me to the ground, and T.J. came up behind him and hit him on the top of the head with his home-made baseball bat. Over the bully fell, out like a light, and the smaller boy headed for home as fast as he could run. The on-lookers started working with the boy who was out cold. He soon awoke, got up, shook his head a few times, and headed home.

This ended our having to take the long route to town. We would strut past those boys' house, and they never came out to the road again when we went by. When school started back that fall, the two boys were back in school, but one thing had changed: there wasn't any more pushing around from these boys.

While we attending Beaverdam School, we lived in a rental house located in what was known as Haunted Hollow. The hollow got its name from being across the road from a graveyard and from the fact that it was in a deep hollow. My Uncle Doyle, the uncle who was running moonshine (the uncle who had taken me for a ride on Thunder Road), came to our house in Haunted Hollow one evening. He had his car loaded with what was called "white-lightning." He had been tipped off that the federal agents had the road blocked leading to a house where he was going to deliver the moonshine. He asked my mother (his sister) if we could hide the "licker" for a while until he could come back and get it.

My mother agreed, although she had no idea about how to hide thirty one-half gallon glass jars of liquid corn. She passed on the job of hiding it to T.J. and me. We got a garden hoe and headed to the corn field near the house and we dug shallow ditches between the corn rows. Next we laid the jars end to end in the rows and covered them with the dirt that we had dug out. But, we had a problem. We had five jars left and no more room in the corn field to put them in, so we started looking for another hiding place.

"How about the hog lot?" T.J. said.

We had a big breeding sow to provide us with pigs for our winter meat supply. Her home, the hog lot, was an enclosure below the spring drain and was a pretty large mud puddle. No one would ever look in that mud for anything, so we pushed the jars out of sight in the mud. The next morning Uncle Doyle came for his moonshine. We found what we had hid in the corn field fairly easy, but when we headed to the hog lot, boy, were we in for a surprise. The old sow had somehow rooted out and broken several jars of Doyle's whiskey. Not only had she broken the jars, she had also had drunk their contents.

We had one of the drunkest hogs that anyone had ever seen. In fact, we had never seen a drunken hog before. She was really happy. She had torn down the fence around the hog lot and was staggering around everywhere. Doyle, T.J., and I finally got her back into the lot, but we didn't find the rest of the moonshine. Doyle loaded up the Ford and made his delivery of the moonshine that was left.

GROWING UP. There were lots of things that I did while growing up that were important to me on the road to becoming an adult. One of the things was the corn shucking that came with the harvest in the fall. All the corn would be piled up near the farmer's corn crib. Word was spread about the time and place of a corn shucking, and all the young people would gather around the pile of corn and begin removing the shucks. If you found an ear that was colored red, you had the privilege of kissing the girl you wanted to give the red ear to. This is what the boys looked for. Sometimes boys brought their own red corn. This was not permitted, so you had to be careful and not get caught. You shucked until midnight and then went into the house for a big feast. It was a custom for all the neighbors' wives to get together and prepare this meal. Corn shucking was an example of neighbors helping neighbors. Lots of other activities like candy pulling, chicken stews, serenading when there was a wedding, square dancing in someone's barn that had a good wooden floor in the loft, and other young peoples' socials were a big part of my life.

My grandma, my daddy's mother, got married a second time. She married a man that everyone called Uncle Tom (Parks). Where he got this name no one seemed to know. I think it was from his appearance.

His hair was snow white and so was the long handlebar mustache he wore. He had no other beard on his face, just the handlebar. I don't know where or how my grandma met Uncle Tom. Grandma lived in Haywood County at Cruso, and Uncle Tom lived in Swain County at Dillsboro. This was quite a distance from Cruso, and the means of communication and travel were very limited, but they did meet somewhere.

Uncle Tom operated a water-wheel-driven corn and grist mill about where the train station is now located in Dillsboro. Another mystery is why he was grinding corn when he had the reputation of being the best and smartest carpenter and woodworker in the country. After he and Grandma Fletcher were married, he moved to Canton where he took over the operation of another water-wheel-driven corn mill. It was located near the Pigeon River at the mouth of Beaverdam Creek. This was a pretty popular meeting place. There were two general merchandise stores along with the corn mill and a one chair barber shop near the mill. One store was owned by Homer Cagle and the other by Glen Moore. The barber shop was operated by Sig McElrath. The barber shop was very popular, not so much for the hair cuts and shaves, but for a place to get the latest news and swap anything from knives to horses. Both of the stores did a good business. You could buy anything that you needed at these stores. This included clothing as well as feed for your livestock. Also, the stores would let their customers buy "on time" (credit) and pay whenever they could. They hardly lost any money because the people that lived in the hollows and hills of Western North Carolina were known for their honesty.

Back to Uncle Tom. I enjoyed visiting him at the corn mill, and I especially liked holding my hands under the steady flow of warm corn meal that came from the stones that were grinding the corn. He always had some sort of story to tell. He eventually closed the mill and moved to Gastonia, North Carolina, where he and my Grandma operated a boarding house for the cotton mill workers. He was known for designing and supervising the building of a beautiful Baptist church there. Some people always looked at Uncle Tom as being a little on the lazy side. Maybe he was just a slow mover. I had other relatives on my Grandma Fletcher's side of the family, but I guess I remember Uncle Tom more than the others.

DIGGING THE WELL. There isn't much that I can add to this chapter. Years later my brother T.J. sent me Conrad's phone number. (Conrad was my partner in the well digging.) He had moved back to the old home place from Florida where he had worked since the beginning of WWII. I called him, and one of the first things he mentioned was the well. I don't think he or I could ever forget this event in our lives. You could only imagine how this happened. I plan to pay Conrad a visit on my next trip to North Carolina.

AN AIRPLANE RIDE. It was a really tough job to skin a frozen steer, especially for us because we had never skinned anything that large. All the experience we had was skinning squirrels, rabbits, possums, and other small animals. Although we got awfully cold, we did the job. It wasn't pretty, but it was done. I have ridden many airplanes over the years, but I remember none of them more vividly than that first one over Asheville, North Carolina.

MODEL A FORD. Owning the Model A Ford was an experience I'll always remember. I didn't spend any money for repairs that the car needed. It only had a little bit of braking power. I usually used the gears to slow the car down. I was reminded of the time I really needed brakes from one the passengers who I hauled to Waynesville when I was working with the NYA. I was visiting in Waynesville, and I was looking through the phone book to see if I recognized any of the names. I saw the name of a Reverend Connard. I called, and sure enough he was one of the ones in the car when I couldn't stop and hit a car full of Yankee tourists. No one was hurt, and there was no serious damage to the other car. I had hit the bumper, but the cars were made for service instead of looks back then. I had one year of use out of the $45 dollar car, and I sold it for $45 dollars.

CCC CAMP. Much thanks to the park superintendent who gave me a ride and some good advice that early Saturday morning. I saw him several times after that, and once he had me drive him to Gatlinburg, Tennessee. This was where the headquarters for the Smokey Mountain camps was. He lived near Cherokee, and I think that one of the several families that still lived in the park supplied him with the moonshine he used for what he called "medicine." I grew up a lot while in the CCC camp.

VIRGINIA. The owner of the company I worked for in Virginia was very good to his employees. He would treat us to a steak dinner or a burlesque show when we worked extra hours. This was in addition to our pay. He would have me come to his home for what he said was business, but I think it was an excuse for him to drink a lot. He liked his beer. His wife didn't care too much for my visits. She sort of blamed me for his drinking. If she said anything to him, we would leave and go to some bar. He never drank enough to be what you would call drunk. He also had a Plymouth car designated as the dating car. He let the boys use it to go on dates with their girlfriends. I liked my living in Virginia.

DRAFTED. I decided I would go into the Army with friends, but it didn't work out that way. All of the ones I grew up with went in different directions after we were given physical exams at Camp Croft in South Carolina. The three months that I was in basic training made a different person of me. There were boys from all over the country in my battery. Most were Yankees, and I suspected a few were former gangsters. Everyone had to take care of himself and not let anyone bully him. The ones from the mountains were called "hillbillies," and we were kidded a lot. They said that we only took a bath once a week. My answer to that was that I took a bath everyday; I just threw the water out once a week

THE WAR. Although there were lots of restrictions in the Army, I enjoyed my few months in England. We moved several times, and I was told later that this was to confuse the Germans. I met lots of nice

English girls. After going to France there wasn't much time for anything not associated with the war. Being in the 3rd Army, we were always traveling in the early part of the war. General Patton, who was the commander of the 3rd Army didn't believe in dragging along; he believed in going forward. The later part of the war, when I was on duty at a POW stockade, I did have some time to enjoy the better things such as they were. I feel lucky that I came back in as good health as I had when I went into the war. I received two campaign medals, one for southern France and one for the Rhineland, which was in Germany. You never forget the things that you see when you go to another country for a war.

GETTING MARRIED. Getting married was a life-time commitment when Marie and I were married. This isn't the case always now. We had some good times and some bad times. We faced everyday challenges as they came. We never had a lot of wealth in terms of money, but we had a wealth of happiness and love for our family. I remember while I was in school in Chicago that we were so short of money that we would buy a twin Popsicle and divide it. The price was only a nickel, but this was splurging for us. We had to pay the rent first and use what was left for food.

RAISING A FAMILY. I guess raising a family is the biggest responsibility that we face in our lives. Not only do we have to make sure we have food on the table and a place to sleep, but we also have the job of being an example for the children in order to shape their future. It's not easy to raise a family, but it is a pleasure. The rewards come many years later when you see your children have a family, and they give you grandchildren who you can be proud of. I can truthfully say that I am proud of the two boys we had and the grandchildren they gave us. Four out of the eight grandchildren have or will be getting a doctorate degree from a university. Not many parents can brag about this achievement. Four out of eight is a pretty good percentage.

MOVING TO TENNESSEE. Moving to Tennessee wasn't too big of a deal for Marie. Most people from large families in the mountain section of North Carolina never wandered too far from where they were born and grew up. There were eight children in the Young family—five girls and three boys. All of them were married and had homes close to where they were born, especially the girls. The boys were in the armed services during or shortly after the WWII. They found out that there was a larger world outside of these mountains.

Anyway, Marie didn't object too much about moving away, so we moved. Her biggest complaint was the difference in the weather. She missed the cool evenings and nights of the mountains. She adjusted pretty well because our children were involved in school, which got her into the action also. Her driving improved so much that she started driving to North Carolina, so she now could visit her family more often. No longer did she have to wait for a weekend when I wasn't working to take her back for a visit, and she didn't have to return to Tennessee at any certain time because of my work. Also, our new house was a plus for her. I guess all women like pretty homes.

THE PAPER MILL. There isn't much that I can say about the paper mill. I went to work and came back home in the evenings if everything was running well. The Engineering Department didn't have much turn over of employees; only a few moved on. I had a couple of opportunities to change jobs, but I didn't change. One of the opportunities was to go back to the mill that I had left to come to Tennessee. They had me come for an interview on a Saturday. Everything went well, and they made me an offer to come back as an employee in their Engineering Department. I probably would have taken the job, but they didn't want to pay me what I was making at Bowater.

Another time I received a call from Allied Paper Mill in Jackson, Alabama. They wanted me to come for an interview for their Electrical Superintendent position. Going there, Marie, Dean, and I took a plane from Chattanooga on a Friday evening, and we stayed on this plane all night. It stopped at every airport in Georgia, Florida, and Alabama. We landed in Mobile at seven the next morning. We had a quick breakfast and got the car that the company had made arrangements for me to drive to Jackson, a trip of about 75 miles. They were at the mill waiting for me. The Mill Manager, Joe Sparks, took Marie and Dean to his home to wait until I was ready to start back home. The interview went well and the money was no problem for them. They wanted me to come to work right away. The mill was new, but the grounds were all a mud hole. It was in a lonely isolated section of Alabama. I had made my decision but told Joe that I would let him know within one week, and we came home. I sent them my expense statement and waited a few days to give them time to reimburse my expenses. I then made a call to Jackson telling them I was not taking the job.

Also, Alleghany Electric Company in Pennsylvania came to see me and offered me a job as Superintendent over the electrical portion of the projects they had going all over the world. The money would have been great, but I would have had to relocate every two or three years as the jobs were completed. The moving part wasn't for Marie or me, so we stayed put.

CLEVELAND. I don't think that I could ever finish all the things that have taken place in my life while living in Cleveland. Some I've already mentioned; some I try to forget. There was a period when I was involved with the country music business. I was co-owner of a recording company. It was called WoodFletch Enterprises, and the recording label was called Arrow Records. We signed about six country artists and even had a couple of recordings in the top ten in the entertainment industry publication *Billboard*. The company could have been successful, but my partner was into drugs, alcohol, and women—you name it, he was doing it all. He was a very talented person when it came to music, though. I let the business fade away.

I then began to do the lighting and sound for the many country music shows that came to Cleveland. I worked on shows starring people like Jerry Lee Lewis (three shows), Farren Young (one show), The Stonemans (two shows), Jack Green (one show), Archie

Campbell (one show), Hank Snow (two shows) and several lesser-known country music groups. I did make a little profit from this venture as well as enjoying this type of work.

I also did some small electrical jobs for friends. I never charged anyone anything for this work.

GRANDCHILDREN. The grandchildren are all grown up now, and all of them are out on their own. Four are married, and four are still in school. One has obtained a PhD, three are studying for their doctorate degrees, two others have completed their bachelor's degrees, and the youngest is studying for a bachelor's degree. One lives in Florida, three live in Tennessee, one lives in Indiana, one lives in Japan, one lives in Colorado, and one lives in Oregon. Ben, who is in Knoxville, comes pretty often to stay with me for the weekend. All the others visit as often as they can. I am proud of all of them as well as my two boys and their wives. All seem to enjoy coming to grandpa's house. I hope that they will always feel welcome at my house.

RETIRED. Except for a few things, I have enjoyed the twenty-three plus years that have passed since leaving Bowater. I built me a small storage building and also two others for my neighbors. I have done several jobs for the church that I attend and numerous small jobs for others. I have never charged anyone for what I do for them. I pray that I will have health and strength to continue helping others.

LIVING ALONE. I have fished some in the past two years. One of my son's best friends, George McCoin, a young attorney, has a lake on the top of a mountain in Polk County that is well stocked with bass, bream, and blue catfish. The only food they get is the soybean fish food. The lake is spring fed, and there is nothing coming into this lake for them to eat, so they must be fed. The catfish have grown, and their numbers have increased so fast that the lake is overstocked. George was told after a survey was done that he needed to take at least two hundred pounds of the catfish out of the lake. He gave me keys to the security gate at his place and asked me to help remove some of the fish, and I have done this. Over the last two years the average weight of the catfish I have taken is around five pounds. They are very clean fish.

On my many trips up Towhee Mountain to the fish pond, I have seen many wild animals such as bear, turkey, pheasant, and deer. On my last trip a wild boar hog tried to attack me. He couldn't reach me because he had been caught in a steel trap somewhere in the mountains and had somehow managed to make it to the lake for water. The rope that was tied to the trap had hung on a tree, and thanks to this he couldn't reach me. Wild hogs in trouble are very dangerous. When going to George's cabin you need to take a gun with you; you never know what wild animals you will encounter or if they will attack you. I don't own a gun, however. I plan on making many more trips to the top of Towhee Mountain, but I will not go alone. If you were hurt or got sick, there isn't anyway to contact someone for help. There are no phones, and it's so isolated that you can't call out on a cell phone. You would be stuck there until George came to feed the fish, and this is only about twice each month.

I don't think I'll ever really get used to living alone. I'll just live day by day and hope for the best. I hope that I will never be a burden to anyone. If I ever lose my independence, I will give up the desire to live. I'll carry on with help from God. He has taken care of me for over eighty-five years, and he knows my needs.